Bugaboo's Secrets

Bugaboo's Secrets

A Noble Stone Adventure In The Okefenokee Swamp

Blake Hendon

Welcome to the Neighborhood! Hope you enjoy —
Blake Hendon
1·19·06

Writers Club Press
New York Lincoln Shanghai

Bugaboo's Secrets
A Noble Stone Adventure In The Okefenokee Swamp

All Rights Reserved © 2002 by Blake Hendon

No part of this book may be reproduced or transmitted in any form or by any means, graphic, electronic, or mechanical, including photocopying, recording, taping, or by any information storage retrieval system, without the written permission of the publisher.

Writers Club Press
an imprint of iUniverse, Inc.

For information address:
iUniverse, Inc.
2021 Pine Lake Road, Suite 100
Lincoln, NE 68512
www.iuniverse.com

Cover photograph of Blake Jr. on his first Okefenokee trip in 1988 taken by the author.
Okefenokee map adapted from U. S. Fish & Wildlife publications by the author.

This is a work of fiction. All events, locations, institutions, themes, persons, characters and plot are completely fictional. Any resemblance to places or persons, living or deceased, are the invention of the author.

ISBN: 0-595-25616-3 (pbk)
ISBN: 0-595-65216-6 (cloth)

Printed in the United States of America

The artist can find in this swamp, scenes for masterpieces—from the beautiful to the somber—for while there are scenes of unsurpassed beauty, there are others, dark, dangerous and foreboding.
—A.S. McQueen and Hamp Mizell
History of Okefenokee Swamp

Wilderness to the people of America is a spiritual necessity, an antidote to the high pressure of modern life, a means of regaining serenity and equilibrium.
—Sigurd Olson

Special thanks go to my wife Barbara, son Blake Jr., daughter Karen and son-in-law Hardegree. I've enjoyed the campfires, trails and eddies we've shared. May there be many more.

Thanks again to my sister Gail for her help and support.

Also, thanks to some Folkston folks: Betty Owens, Maggie O'Connell and Greg Blanks. Thirty-something others deserve recognition and thanks for their work in keeping most of the 438,000 acres in the Okefenokee a National Wilderness Area. It's a beautiful place.

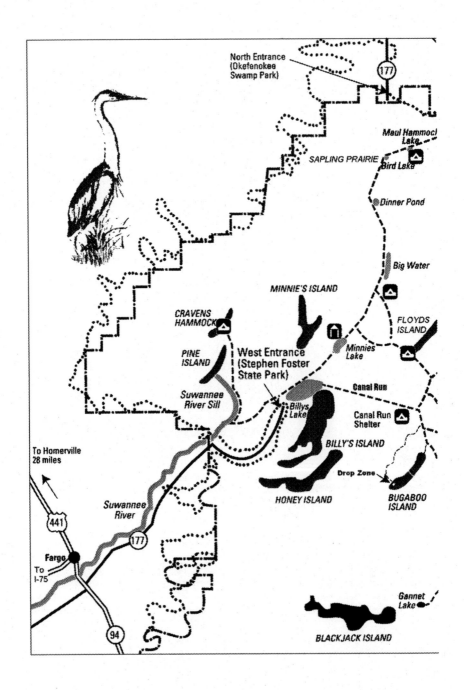

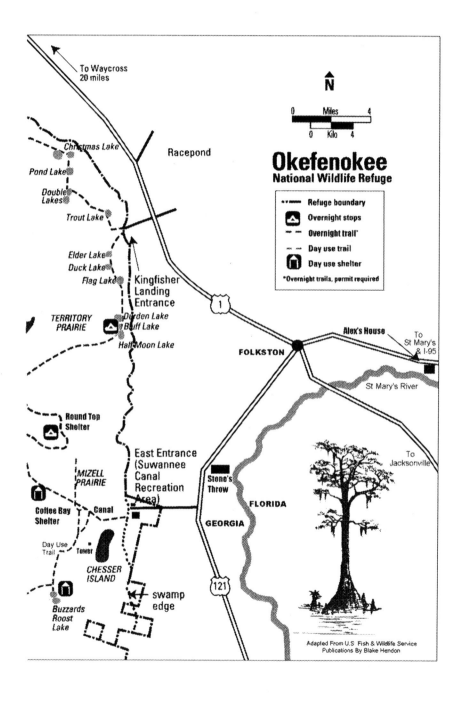

Chapter 1

I could tell we were being followed even when the trailing car and its occupants changed as we cruised through Macon. The first crew must have started out with us in Athens. The shift changed after only eighty miles—two men in a dark fleet-style car with heavily tinted windows. I didn't think it changed in Cordele, which was the next town over ten thousand in population, but it might in Tifton if town size had anything to do with it. I wasn't normally in the habit of checking for tails but I guess it came naturally if you read a lot of fiction and especially if you fudge a little on the speed limit.

Whoever was behind the surveillance had to be big-time despite the ease in spotting their hired help. To have placed the pursuing teams so close together on the route to South Georgia took planning, personnel, and vehicles, and such an undertaking could only have been spawned by the government, a major corporation, or a crime faction. Another country might have been the source of all the attention, but they would likely have been working through the politics, business, and criminal elements they had already infiltrated or controlled in this our great country…a country where my fantasies run wild, thanks to libraries, book stores and real life high adventure, where the coals of my imagination are fanned a constant white-hot.

The surveillance seemed like a wasted effort to me. It was no secret that we were driving down to Folkston to the annual Stone Family reunion—a sociable, non-threatening endeavor. A two-night canoe trip and four more days of R and R were no big deal either, but I certainly didn't feel obligated to make a public announcement telling strangers of my comings and goings. Those guys had gotten my itinerary from someone else.

Maybe I was flattering myself that I was deserving of such attention and was simply building up the scenario in my mind to make things interesting like a James Patterson yarn. I probably did that sometimes, but in reality I usually ended up being right—like James' and my fictional hero, Alex Cross.

Not many people really gave a rat's rear about Noble Stone and my goings on other than those interested in a timely payment of my rent and bills and an appropriate amount of time devoted to foreplay, afterglow and non-sports television. These things made my value go up and the recipients considered me worthy of their favor until such time as my funds and services again came due. Hampton Wormant, asleep next to me, got his once a month in the form of rent and Bonnie Gill, probably asleep next to her carpool driver headed for Saturday work, got hers twice a week in the form of sexual diversion if I (or she) was lucky. Any more would likely be deemed unnecessary by both my housemate and my girlfriend, though I was fully capable of performing my financial and, in her words, feral responsibilities more often if the need arose.

Actually, I had friends, and especially family, that cared about me. It's just that I never liked to use the word "friend" loosely. Also, "good" should never have to be used with it because there shouldn't be different grades of friends—either you are or you aren't. It would be like grading rainbow splendor. In fact, how can you have good friends if there's no such thing as bad friends? The single word said it all.

Mom always said friendships have to be cultivated and maintained. I disagreed. There had never been enough of me to create a great network of friends and constantly keep up to date with them. Folks can live a big part of their life without me bugging them all the time. I can be absent from, or out of touch with, true friends for long periods of time, but when we were back together it was like no time had passed. Sure, we did some catching up and comparing notes, but it was not a critical part of our reunion. We just resumed a natural bond that kept us tuned together despite the occasional interference of agenda or locale. We all change, but there was still that core in us not unlike the family tie of blood that kept us together, at least in our mind and soul.

So, people did care about me and I cared about them on a varying scale just like most of us would care about the environment or mankind. I just didn't call all of them friends. Few of us would fit in the category of a true activist or pacifist in such worthy causes but, instead, in that category in the middle where the paint was worn the most. I'd felt for a long while that good hard honest work in any field was just as rewarding and fulfilling as a sharply focused crusade. If all work were done right and honestly, there wouldn't be as great a need to lead or join a cause other than maybe a religious one if the narrow-mindedness and rigidity didn't drive you away.

All that said, rather than have a category "three" friend, I looked to words like acquaintance, colleague, teammate, dance partner or fellow traveler without wearing out the word "friend." Look what happened to the word "love."

Hampton, or Hamp for short, my sleeping fellow traveler, was also my friend. He was my housemate, landlord, a lawyer, and maker of endless repair lists for a grand old gingerbread home on Milledge Avenue in Athens, Georgia. Add to those descriptions a very lucky person to have had me and my construction service company handy to work on the lists with little or no cost or delay. What a bargain. I couldn't complain, though, because my rent was little more than half the utilities which, for two knuckle-dragging guys with somewhat dulled sensibilities, was not much considering what they would be if the other gender monitored the comfort levels for everyone in every room. We didn't even turn on the heat last winter until we started seeing our breath.

Hamp's needs, like mine, were few. Give him a phone jack and a receptacle for a surge protector and his Compaq Presario would splice him into hours of data-diversion unless there was a football game on TV or his girlfriend diverted him.

"'Bout ready for breakfast?" I asked when he shifted slightly in his seat. It was, in fact, his seat because we were in his Range Rover, an $80,000 piece of status I wouldn't mind having, but couldn't justify. My ride was a nice burgundy GMC pickup with a crew cab and fully loaded with options, construction tools, and equipment—the latter two from a big basement job I had just finished the day before and actually got paid for in full. Rather than unload everything and drive it south, I told Hamp I would drive if we took his car. It ended up a double score for me since I like to drive the black beauty. I shouldn't have made that arrangement while he was thought-bound on the Internet, but he remembered agreeing when he saw the coffee cups, food wrappers and material receipts on the floor and seat of the pickup he would have occupied and the dusty tools on the back seat where his luggage would have been.

"Yep."

Hamp Wormant was sometimes a man of few words, which was fine with me. The ones that talk a lot don't end up saying much anyway. We'd been friends since high school, way back when some of us got away with calling him Wormy, so thankfully I could interpret the true meaning of his brief replies and take action if required. In that case, what he really said was, "Hell yes, I'm about to starve to death and if you don't find food right away, I'll kick your ass."

That was what I got out of the speed of reply, choice of words, inflection, and brevity. If he had said, "I guess," he could have waited a while longer; if he had said, "Whenever you're ready," he was not hungry, but could always eat something. I eased on up to eighty to speed things up a little.

In an effort to get his mind off food deprivation, I said, "We've been followed since I-20, that I'm aware of."

He straightened slightly in his seat, but said nothing. He didn't even look behind us.

My needs, like Hamp's, were few. I used the customary lull in the conversation to reflect that if I had a room big enough to store all my books, a cubbyhole for my photographic equipment, and a proper light bulb in each, I had reached nirvana unless sidetracked by a TV basketball game or Bonnie, if either was in season. Sometimes I watched football with Hamp, but didn't consider it rough enough for the players considering all the protective gear they wore and the soft surface they had to fall on.

"Are we going to be shot at again?" he finally said as he stared ahead.

I was glad the conversation was on a roll but resented where it was going. "Damn, Hamp, the guy was robbing a convenience store. I thought since you helped by bringing him down you agreed he should be stopped."

"I was trying to stop the shooting of bullets after you ticked him off."

"I only asked what the hell he thought he was doing."

"Sure—from behind merchandise," he said simply. "I was right behind him."

"I provided a distraction so you could tackle him."

"We should have had a plan. The cop said we were stupid."

I had gotten a little flustered. "He would have said that if we had a plan. Look, next time, one of us will distract the bad guy while the other overcomes him. That will be the plan."

I couldn't hold back any longer and started laughing. Hamp joined in. That close range episode used to be a real sore spot for him, but now we just laughed it off. There were other encounters, too, and I knew he would bring up at least one when the laughter died down. He did.

"Both of us distracting that guy in the park was not a good plan either, Noble. Especially after the way you provoked him. Calling him butt-ugly would rile anyone."

"Yeah, but at least the jogger got away."

"And I got shot."

Hamp was grazed on the right hip by a bullet as we both ran in a wild and distracting manner from the lady's provoked and armed, we came to find out, assailant. There were no trees nearby for me to hide behind and distract alone.

"You should have gone to the doctor," I finally managed, validating my concern for his health.

"There would have been a police report and that same cop might have been dispatched to make it. He would have arrested us for being stupid twice."

"You're probably right," I agreed reluctantly. "Any body else would have gotten a medal or at least a citation for bravery. The jogger didn't even thank us for saving her."

Most of our adventures were not completely my doing. Hamp could get us in fixes just by effecting his own brand of solutions that weren't completely thought out. Also, yarn spinner Clive Cussler and another of my fictional heroes, Dirk Pitt, should share some of the blame. Somehow they brought out my adventurous spirit.

I had gotten off I-75 onto the Tifton exit. The sign a mile back promised four fast food places. "McDonald's OK?"

"Yep."

I sped up a little but Hamp said, "Stop by that auto parts place first." He was looking toward the rear at our followers getting on the exit ramp.

"I thought you were hungry."

He didn't say anything. Oh, shit. Maybe he was going to eat a moon hubcap to tide him over for the next .7 miles. I pulled in and parked. He was back in no time, pocketing his change and something in a small blister package. I had the Range Rover turned around and the motor running when he got in.

"That them?" Hamp asked and clicked his eyes once up to the deceleration lane that led to the parts place.

I looked up and my A-hole tightened reflexively. There were two identical dark blue cars with two identical men in dark clothing and shades occupying each of them. The tinted windows made the dim shapes even more ominous. One of the matched set must have been the team that we picked up in Macon and the other was probably their replacement stationed there in Tifton, if that was the way it worked. I told this to Hamp as we pulled out on the road. I also added, "This is not a result of something you've gotten into, is it?" just to get the heat off me before he started blaming me.

There was a pregnant pause before he calmly spoke. Then, "Noble, I'm a corporate lawyer, not a criminal one, so I don't give cause for people who are dressed and motor-pooled for the occasion to follow me 320 miles to your family's—my adopted family's—enjoyable reunion on a lazy, early spring weekend in rural South Georgia. I don't question people with guns in a distracting manner either. Also, Sally Haleman is of age and consents to my advances and carnal gains. The only marks against me are a few unfair speeding and parking tickets that I dutifully paid for, and painting something on the Tech Coliseum Dome. All things considered, I'm still pure as the goddamned fucking driven snow and this is something that you, as always, have gotten us into."

I was beaming as I parked Black Beauty on the right side of Mickey D's. Hamp could distribute some words when inspired, and I guess I did back him into a corner. He was probably hell in a courtroom, or wherever he performed, though I knew that the past week he'd worked quietly at home preparing for a big corporate merger before we left for our week off down South.

We lingered in the car until the dark blues rolled around to the back of the building. After they passed, we went inside and to the right and took turns going to the restroom while the other watched the car. Three of the men entered on the opposite side from us and the fourth strolled toward the Rover, but put his hand to his ear as if receiving a message and looked up and saw me looking out the window. He went back around the building and entered the side his buddies had moments before. There was something we had with us they wanted.

I admit that my heart rate was pushing a hundred, but I figured Hamp's was hovering around his nearly-asleep sixty to seventy and he would provide stability to our twosome. After I washed up and we walked to the counter to order, I noticed our four followers sitting in a corner booth on the opposite side we went in on, drinking Cokes and probably comparing notes before passing the baton. With our Big Breakfasts, we sat in their full view on the side of the building we entered to make their job easier and also to keep an eye on them and the car.

Between mouthfuls, I said, "They look too pure to be mob—must be some federal agency with three letters." I immediately wished I hadn't said that. I was bad about making casual, bordering on flippant, remarks in serious situations to hide my apprehension. That peeved Hamp to no end.

He looked up at me, but was still thoughtfully and quietly chewing, which counted for something. Translated, he said, "You son of a bitch. You drag me off under the guise of a family outing and here we are pursued by three-lettered feds or possibly criminal elements and if I get shot in the ass again, you can kiss yours goodbye." After swallowing, what he actually said aloud was, "I think you need to start explaining things."

I really didn't think Hamp would harm me badly. I'm not even sure he could win in a fair scuffle, though he stayed in good shape, considering his occupation. The only time we fought with any determination was over who was going to lose his innocence first with Lainey Delbeck. We were like rutting mammals. The fight was a draw, but I had gotten seconds because of a coin toss. We should have done that to begin with because we were both bloody pulps, but that's hindsight.

I kept pretty fit too, but *because* of my occupation. I got a daily workout on my construction projects while Hamp went to a fitness club twice a week and walked from the far end of his parking lot at work. We both ran at least three times a week to the arch at UGA and back. That was only two and a half miles round trip, but the route included parts of some of the seven hills of Athens. It was enough to make even Hamp's heart rate tachycardic.

We both had decent muscles, though I considered mine harder and more sinuous. At twenty-eight, two months apart, we looked pretty good. I was a fuzz taller than his six foot, one inch, but we both hovered around one eighty. My face was thinner and more tanned with the Stone family Protestant nose, high cheeks and brown eyes, while Hamp sported a slightly fuller face with a strong chin and a straight nose that divided gray-blue eyes. At one time, he had a thick, reddish-tinted mustache and beard, but shaved them off after the park incident to avoid being recognized by the lady jogger's assailant, should he still have been around. I got by with patchy two day-old facial hair growth because of my macho work, but I cleaned up nicely, as they say, when necessary.

Hamp kept his dark hair short with a neat part, while my lighter brown hair could fall in my eyes unless brushed just so without a definite part. Bonnie kept me posted on when I needed a haircut.

"Hamp, if I knew anything, I would tell you. Cousin Chase called Tuesday and seemed concerned about something he saw. He wanted to be sure we were going to the reunion and on the swamp trip, and reminded me to bring the enlarged photos I developed for him. He didn't want to say any more on the phone, which was a little strange, but I'm sure it has nothing to do with us. I haven't really felt watched at home, but I don't go checking from window to window either. Other than the obvious surveillance on the way down, that's all I know."

Hamp finished eating before I did, and said, "I've got to pee again. Wait here and I'll come back and we'll leave together." That said volumes.

I got a refill of Coke under watchful eyes and returned to the booth to finish my hash browns. It was nearly ten minutes before Hamp returned.

"Ready?" he said as he walked up. *Let's get the hell out of here, quick.*

The unsaid words caused me to stand quickly and prepare to bolt, but I had the presence of mind to follow Hamp's lead and took my tray and trash to the container. My legs partially locked up and caused my strides to be slightly stiff and jerky. Knowing eight eyes behind dark shades were on us gave me a self-conscious, stage-frighty sensation and caused my motor ability to partially default. In another similar situation, Hamp said the word for that was "cataplexy." Hell, "scared shitless" has one less syllable.

He maintained his usual post-coital temperament.

We returned to I-75 south without incident. After three miles, I realized we weren't being followed anymore.

Chapter 2

▼

"Were you really in on that?"

"What?" Hamp replied. He finished his Coke with a wet clatter.

"Painting 'I DREAMED...' on the Tech dome."

I remembered reading about it when we still shared an apartment. We had both graduated at Georgia but Hamp wanted to get into law. I saved up to get in construction in spite of my business degree. The newspaper article reported that in the late fifties, the Maidenform Brassiere Company had an ad campaign that pictured a beautiful, well-formed woman in appropriate attire and setting saying things like, "I dreamed I went to the ball in my Maidenform Bra," or, "I dreamed I saw Rome in my Maidenform Bra." The Tech Coliseum had been finished during that time and some engineering students were quick to pick up on its form despite the lack back then of female students to help with a mental picture and painted the two familiar words, "I DREAMED..." in twelve inch thick letters on the dome facing the I-75/I-85 corridor through Atlanta. The daring, and I admit, enterprising deed was repeated, according to the article, over forty years later when its meaning was not likely understood by many, and its sexual overtone long diluted by a more tolerant society.

Hamp looked at me and smiled. "Some fellow law students and I were in Atlanta to take the bar exam and the last night we were there, we decided to go on a lark, which included getting the paint and roller to repeat the performance Dad had planned and carried out with his buddies when he was at Tech in the fifties. The three of us pulled it off again without a hitch, thanks to Dad's frequent recounts of the caper to me since my childhood. The parking lot and fencing were different from his descriptions but they, or his recollection, could have changed over the years and it didn't pose a problem.

"I called Dad when we got back to the hotel at 3:00 a.m. and had to give my account of the adventure three times before he was sure he had all the details. He didn't ask about the bar exam. I found out later that after we hung up, he dressed immediately and drove from Charlotte to Atlanta to get pictures of the 'lonely tit,' as it was called, in the morning sun. An enlarged print is framed and hanging in his den. The pictures in the newspapers were not suitable for framing, but they are in his scrapbook."

"How come you never told me about that?" I was disappointed that I was not included in the prank and even more let down that he never mentioned it to me.

He didn't answer. Sure, I would have told everybody I knew about it and maybe the tip that I told in confidence could have reached unforgiving authorities, but you never know. Judging by his dreamy look, I figured the event was a father/son rite of passage thing that I would never breach unless someone specifically asked me if I was privileged to know who could have pulled off such a glorious feat. Then I would have spilled my guts.

We were halfway between Tifton and Waycross and I couldn't stand it any longer. "I wonder why we aren't being followed any more?" Hamp had spent an inordinate amount of time in the restroom back at McDonald's and I somehow equated that to the lack of the tail, which was always the constant mile or so behind us. He has spent less time in the john even when armed with a magazine—porno or otherwise.

"They have flat tires."

"Both of them?" I was referring to cars.

"All eight of them." He was referring to tires.

My sphincter tightened again. Without need to closely analyze the situation, I said, "Damn, Hamp, that's not going to make any problem go away. Talk about *me* provoking people. Did you think this out completely?" If he had, he was a quick thinker like me.

There was no pregnant pause. "Those guys were in my wake, Noble, which I consider part of my space and I choose who I share it with. There are also laws against clandestine surveillance, and until they confront us with ID or AK-47's so I know where we stand, I can play cat and mouse with them 'til the fucking cows come home. I'm just calling their hand."

That was clear, and all of it aloud, but I still had to say, "Jesus."

We didn't pick up another tail in Waycross, so the one in Tifton having his valve stems and air replaced must have been assigned to us all the way to Folkston. Hamp had pulled from his Duckheads eight valve stems and the extractor bought at the parts store, which corroborated his story. The act shouldn't be considered a major theft, especially since air is free, but there were some pissed off good or bad guys that I felt were eventually going to call *our* hand.

We made it to Folkston by 1:30 and had a quick burger at the Dairy Queen before weaving our way through the small town Saturday traffic to the Charlton County sheriff's office at the end of Main Street. It was in a corner office of the stately 1928 courthouse building on the first floor. The dispatcher, jail, and other space required for the day-to-day law enforcement operation was in a separate building two hundred feet from the side entrance where we were headed. Maggie the dispatcher, waved from a plate glass window in the smaller building and picked up the phone. By the time we stretched our legs and walked up the time-worn marble steps to the glass door, my Cousin Jar was unlocking the door.

* * * *

Mason "Jar" Jarrett was six years my senior at thirty-four, and had been sheriff for three and a half years. He was the county's youngest sheriff ever and a good one. He was my dad's sister's third son and the only one of them to remain near his place of birth, which I guessed was OK. His mother even moved to Jacksonville to live with a sister when Uncle Jes died. Armed with a degree in criminal justice, he could have found work in most any city or state but chose to stay in Folkston. Sometimes I think that if everyone chose not to leave their hometown, an area could become clogged with folks of the same blood, and there would be no room for outsiders. Some swampers can crank out the kin and if no one left, my hometown would be no place for the huddled masses. It has been said that Okefenokee people since the Seminoles, and even the race of giants that preceded them, lived unusually long lives. They say that it was in the water. This would farther exacerbate the overpopulation problem if we didn't spread out and improve the world around us like I did. Hamp's entire family left after his dad's engineering work in the area played out, so they did their part too.

Jar was 200 pounds of short, thick gristle. There was little flab on him if by mischance he was seen naked, but with clothes on, he might have seemed overweight. His penchant for the fats, oils and sweets at the "use-sparingly" tip of the food pyramid could have been some of the problem, but his short stature helped with that misperception too. On our yearly paddling trips, he was usually in the canoe with Cousin Chase, who weighed only 160.

Jar's round head sat directly on his shoulders, and his military haircut left a round copper-colored mat of hair only on the very top that might remind someone of the lid of a Mason jar if they saw his body mass at the same time. Hence, his nickname. Mason, his first name, used along with an abbreviated version of his last helped make it stick.

Years ago, Jar took it on his own to explain to me the endless and baffling mysteries that cropped up on my journey into and through puberty. I was able to pass on to my awed peers, who relied mostly on their dads, the amazing things of life that were available to a young male that I gained freely from my learned cousin without asking. I could have taken over a small country with my following of young men eager to learn and try things explained so formally and forbiddingly by their parents. Later, Hamp was directly offered such wisdom by Jar as we became friends. Outings with Jar promised new insight for us into the social and economic games we must play. Sex and dating were always the hottest topics, but advice and techniques on many things such as ingenious pranks, smoking, drinking, fighting, sports, and even grooming and style were offered as well. By the end of high school, we had put to the test much of what was available to a small town young man without wrecking our car with dirty underwear on or going blind from a favorite pastime. We never tried drugs, though, and had to thank Jar for that. Jar had turned out two smoke- and drug-free, tattoo- and piercing-free citizens, and he was proud of us. Secretly, I had always wanted to have a nipple pierced, but Bonnie helped me be strong by offering her opinion on that.

*   *   *   *

Jar hugged us both and turned his key to re-lock the door before leading us to the far end of the corridor and through an open door. He had apparently been attacking a sub sandwich and a twelve-ounce bag of barbecue potato chips while poring over correspondence and posters before we arrived. Lois Sickle, his secretary and a friend of my mom's, was off on Saturday and not there to greet us, but would probably be at the reunion. The office space was cavernous and voices echoed accordingly. It had no anteroom or partitions for privacy and openly housed Jar's and Lois' desks, filing cabinets and other essentials including a coffee maker that served offices on that end of the corridor.

Though unmarried, Jar always looked and smelled like he had just shaved and showered. He faithfully wore starched and perfectly pressed khakis and for that particular Saturday, he sported a blue polo shirt and new boat shoes and matching leather belt. He seemed ever mindful that some day he would attract and take into custody a good wife with the help of careful grooming and they would have little half-pint Jars. He looked up and his meaty face allowed a warm smile with no accompanying wrinkles.

"You guys made good time," he said. He sat on the edge of his desk and raised his trouser legs slightly to protect the crease.

"We got an early start," I replied. "I figured Mom and Dad might need help getting set up for tomorrow. On the phone she talked like there was a lot to do."

"They've been working hard for at least two weeks, so everything seems to be in good shape. Of course, they would never say that. It's at the point now where things are starting to get redone. It's like that every year. Chase is at the funeral home now to borrow folding chairs, though I don't think we will need them. We never do."

My parents provided the site for the reunion since they owned a motor home and camping park between Folkston and the Suwannee Canal recreation area. It was a central location for the rolling Stones in Florida and Georgia to make it in one day. For most, the trip was under two hours, though some came from as far as Texas and Louisiana and arrived a day or two early to rest from the trip.

Two cousins, Ty and Byron Slappey, from Memphis had a long drive. They would be joining us for the first time on our annual canoe trip after the reunion if they didn't have car trouble like they did last year. They owned a used car business together with Uncle Graham and always drove their best vehicle down with hopes that it would make the trip. Dad always said they weren't the brightest bulbs on the car lot sign but I reserved judgment since we never hung out together before they moved.

The eighteen-acre camping park had a playground, a small in-ground swimming pool for the kids, a good-sized covered pavilion with baths, rest rooms and picnic tables, and a one-acre fishing pond. A small pasture doubled as a softball field and two sets of deep horseshoe-wallowed pits claimed the all-day shaded areas. The volleyball court was near the pavilion to entertain the older Stones and to draw their cheers. The early arrivals came on the Friday or Saturday before the big event to enjoy the activities, visit with kin, or spend the day at nearby Suwannee Canal. They camped overnight at Mom and Dad's "Stone's Throw Park."

The get-together was always the weekend nearest the full moon in April. The bright nights gave extra time for the kids to have fun outdoors and wear down for bedtime while the grownups talked. For those lucky enough to get overnight camping permits in the swamp like we were this time, the nighttime light and shadows controlled by the great buttery sphere were unforgettable, especially at Round Top Shelter, our first night's stop on the canoe trail. Our second night would be on land at Floyd's Island. The month of April was a good time for such outings and our family get-togethers because the heat and insects were not yet a major problem. Black flies during the day and mosquitoes at night were just starting to be pesky and, along with deer flies, would become unbearable without repellent as the warmer weather eased in.

"Ready for the swamp?" Jar asked.

"I brought plenty of South African wine and Jamaican Blue Mountain coffee, if that's what you mean," Hamp answered with a grin. He always took creature comforts a step farther on such trips with exceptional wine and thirty-five dollar a pound coffee and the splurges possibly kept us from reverting to savagery. "I hope you and Chase took care of the food and gear like before, or I need to go shopping."

"I have money to settle up with, my camera, and personal gear," I added. "What's left?"

"Looks like we're set, then." Jar moved around behind his desk and picked up a Post-it note. "Your neighbor Freddie called an hour ago and wanted one of you to call. He sounded like a pretty decent sort."

Hamp and I glanced at each other. *Shit. What could it be?*

I was closest, so I took the note with the number. "He's an Athens-Clarke County cop, so I'm sure you gravitated toward him," I said. "We told him about you and some of our least incriminating adventures."

I dialed the number and Freddie Pope picked up after the first ring.

"Glad you got my message," he began. "I didn't have your folks' first name or number and didn't want to worry them with a call anyway, but I knew your lawman cousin could find you.

"Ya'll didn't hire a security service for the time you are away, did you?"

"Not with you next door. What's going on?"

Freddie rented the basement apartment in the house next to Hamp's and we three usually got together when his wife had her biweekly nights out.

"I was walking the dog just after you guys left this morning and found two men snooping around your place checking doors and windows. I confronted them and they flashed security ID and said they were checking on the place. I flashed *my* ID and they looked a little nervous. When I asked them if they would wait while I called you or Hamp, they said they were done and had rounds to make and they left in a hurry. I couldn't detain them without good cause, but I know they were up to no good."

"Freddie, I think those were bad guys. We were followed down here by two different teams in dark blue cars until Hamp disabled them. There's probably a connection."

"What do you think they want?"

"We don't know. I'm pretty sure it has to do with something down here, but apparently there's something at home too. Wouldn't a tracking device on Hamp's car have been easier than following us?"

"The equipment is readily available and most security and surveillance companies have it. I think they simply didn't want you out of their sight and were taking no chances. Since they haven't approached you yet, they might just want to keep track of you while looking for something at your house. It does seem like overkill though."

A thought occurred to me. "Freddie, do you still have the key to the house?"

"Sure."

"There's a single cardboard drawer-box marked 'Swamp Negatives' in my darkroom. Would you get it and hang on to it? I think those guys will visit us again and we won't be there to welcome them. If they do, they won't be so open about it this time and will wait until dark."

"I'll call my captain and get more frequent cruiser patrols. I'm off this weekend and we're going out for dinner tonight, but when we get back, I'll keep an eye out."

"We appreciate that, Freddie. If we find out anything down here, we'll let you know." I gave him my folks' number in case he had to call again. "By the way, what was the name of their company?"

"Safepoint Security.

"Hey, Noble?"

"Yeah?"

"Can I borrow *Bambi and Heidi Do Dixie*?"

"Sure," I answered with a smile. "It's in the video rack. I'll have to tell Cindy, though."

"She likes the part with the farmhand."

"Oh…bye, Freddie."

"Bye."

Jar had followed my side of the conversation with interest but his attention suddenly turned to the open door to the office. While still talking, I followed his line of sight to the floor and thought I caught movement of a faint shadow near the door's hinge side. By the time I hung up, Jar had made his way quietly to the opening, keeping to the side. He put his right index finger to his lips, then reached around the jamb with his thick curly orange-haired arm and pulled hard in an arc. A figure in a dark suit and sunglasses followed the arm into the room, banging hard against the strike side of the jamb before continuing in a blur with the freckled arm and slamming to the floor face down.

Chapter 3

I cringed reflexively, knowing it had to have hurt the guy. Jar placed his right knee to the middle of the guy's back and put his weight on it while gathering two unresisting arms together.

"Cuffs," he said simply, and jerked his head to his gun belt on the coat rack.

Hamp grabbed them and handed them over while I still stared in disbelief.

"Jesus, God!" the figure screamed. "What in the hell do you think you are you doing!"

Jar started to turn him over but hesitated when he touched the man's side. He reached under his coat and pulled out a black automatic handgun. "Check his ankles, Noble."

I patted down his ankles like I knew what I was doing while Jar turned him over. I found a small caliber pistol in a holster above his right ankle and removed it.

"Son of a bitch!" Jar said when he took off the man's shades. "Gus Bunner, what the fuck are you doing sneaking around here?"

"Get these goddamned cuffs off me, Jarrett. You have stepped in some serious shit now." He spoke with a haughty roar despite his predicament.

Jar reached in the guy's inside coat pocket. "I'm going to check your ID first to be sure FBI is not misspelled by the Cracker Jack people. That is, if the FBI is still putting up with you. I can't believe you are sneaking around outside my office in a locked courthouse. Who authorized this and why didn't they call me first?"

"This is routine surveillance, Jarrett, and in case you've forgotten, we can work in your county." He had gathered what composure he could and replaced his grating bray with equally irritating grunted words as he spoke.

"Like when you and your misguided ATF buddies raided Buddy Brant's home? Christ, Bunner, he had receipts and registration on all those guns. He has a license to carry and to sell too." Jar got to his feet but didn't offer to help him up.

"Our information indicated he had illegal firearms. We've since taken care of the slip-up. Now get me out of these cuffs." His tone was cooling down but you could still light matches on him without striking.

Bunner struggled to his feet without help and maintained his sneer. He stood about six feet, most of it in stilt-like legs. His pants didn't break on his shoes and I figured his off-the-rack suit's inseam maxed at the length he wore. The way he labored to stand, he might not have been in the best of shape for the mid-forties, but in all fairness, he still had the handcuffs on to hinder him. He glared at Hamp and me through cold, ice-blue eyes as if we were the intruders. Every mousy brown hair on his head was still in place after the quick trip through the door and down to the floor and I wondered how much hair spray it took to withstand those forces.

"Slip-up?" Jar looked in disbelief. "That was no slip-up. That was a stupid, careless, thoughtless mistake and there couldn't be any possible excuse for it. You and your men completely destroyed Buddy's front and back doors along with their frames and scared the shit out of him and Vickie. What if one of them had had a heart attack? You guys are unbelievable."

"Jarrett, if you don't get these handcuffs off me, I'm going to report you."

"Report me to whom? To the people that elected me to this office? The same people that raised hell to their senator until you guys paid for the damage to Buddy and Vickie Brant's house? I'm the one that's going to do some reporting unless you tell me what the fuck you are doing here. We may be a small town off the beaten path but we have some easily-heard politicians that will worry the piss out of your boss."

Jar unlocked the cuffs and allowed Bunner to retrieve his guns and ID. He changed his tone a little and continued. "Bunner, I need to know if we should start locking our doors. I have a responsibility here and if you go getting close-mouthed over something I should be sandbagging for, then we're not doing our jobs. Christ, man, we're on the same side."

"We are monitoring certain activities of Safepoint Security in Georgia and Florida," Gus Bunner said, "and noticed a particular interest they had in following Mr. Stone and Mr. Wormant here from Athens. Right now, that's all I'm authorized to tell you. If we need your help at a future date, we'll contact you. I might warn you that some of Safepoint's dealings stretch lawful pursuits a bit and involvement with them will be suspect." His eyes clicked from Hamp to me.

I knew Jar was pissed but he didn't let it show. I also knew Hamp was holding back but I couldn't tell from his body language for how long. It was like this Bunner guy was condemning Hamp and me along with our stalkers. Jeez. I just hoped Hamp would let Jar handle the guy and not provoke him. I was the one that usually did the provoking, but I was kind of enjoying the exchange and watching Jar in action. I had no intention of riling a fed whose hands were now free and his holsters full. Jar had been doing a good job of stirring him up anyway.

"I'm authorized to tell you," Jar began, "that if you need any help in this county you can stick your head up your ass and see if you can find some. That's how much help you would give me. I also suggest that you buy a cute farm animal to take home with you for companionship and that you and your misdirected buddies, who are surely lurking nearby, get out of Charlton County before one of you pees on an electric fence and causes chaos. You guys might also try to remember that the best way to get through a barbed-wire fence is to go to the gate. Even then, watch out for the bull, which is me if you know what a metaphor is."

"I don't know if your complaint is with me or the Bureau, Jarrett, but our work is important and you need to remember we carry a lot of weight."

Jar sighed in submission. Nothing he said was understood or retained by Bunner.

Jar said, "On your way out of town, stop by Buddy Brant's gun and knife museum that he just opened up across from the Chamber of Commerce. It's the largest private collection in Georgia and it's open until four on Saturdays. You won't have to break the door down but it costs four bucks—cheaper than paying for a door, I guess."

* * * *

After Bunner left, we sat in peaceful silence while contemplating the significance of the FBI snooping around Folkston. Hamp and I had left the Safepoint surveillance boys in Tifton and I had all but written off any farther threat from them since their team in Athens was confronted by Freddie Pope and we had reached our destination with what I thought they were after. They would either have to change tack or change course or quit. The FBI's interest in them had definitely started to give more gravity to the situation and I had started to develop a pretty good theory.

Jar broke the silence and spoke to me. "Chase mentioned some shots he took that you were going to develop. Did you bring the prints?"

"They're in the Range Rover. Want to see them?"

"Might ought to. This could be serious even if Bunner's methods are a joke. Besides, if we go to Stone's Throw now, we'll be aimlessly shuffling chairs and tables around for Hank and Dottie." He chose a thick commercial duty key on his bulky ring and handed the whole thing to me.

Henry and Dorothy were my parents. They always worked hard on preparations for the family gathering, trying to make it special for my grandparents, great-grandparents, and great-great-grandparents. Grandmomma, as she did with many of our clan's newcomers, helped birth me under the watchful eye of Granny, her mother, and Momma Dessie, her grandmother. There were perfectly good hospital facilities in Folkston, but traditions seemed to perpetuate better when the lives of ancestors overlapped for longer periods so the customs could be ingrained for succeeding generations. Home births were so natural for those with Stone blood that no one bothered to question them.

All the head Stones lived within eight miles of one another and, despite their age, would drive their own cars to Mom and Dad's early on Sunday morning and make a full day of it. Saturday nights were reserved for the young adults, forty and under, and their shenanigans. There was no drinking on Sunday unless it was sneaked.

As I started out to the parking lot, Hamp asked me to bring a scrap of paper on the Rover's console with two tag numbers on it. I should have known.

I stepped out into the bright sunlight and froze when I saw a figure shading his eyes and peering into the Rover. I started to deliver my provoking line even without Hamp, but recognized the Suwannee Canal tee shirt and sun-streaked hair of cousin Chase. His broad shoulders and arms shaped the upper part of the shirt, but the lower part was loose and untucked. Dad's old Chevy pickup was nearby, loaded with folding chairs.

"Hey, Bud," I said after I got closer.

Chase spun around and the shading hands became fists, but when he saw who I was, his hands spread open. He was embarrassed by his reaction. Before lowering them, we hugged. Most Stones, male or female, were huggers.

"You OK?" I asked.

"Sure," he said automatically. Then, "Well, not exactly." His copper-brown eyes clicked left, then right, as if looking for eavesdroppers. He looked burdened and vulnerable.

"Let's go inside. Jar and Hamp are there. We need to talk."

"No, wait. I don't want Jar to know this. I think my place was broken into Wednesday night."

His "place" was a remodeled twenty-six foot 1962 Airstream Overlander Land Yacht parked in a private space at Stone's Throw. He could have stayed at his parents' home in town, but he liked the independence he had enjoyed since leaving for college five years ago. Also, he worked at Suwanee Canal and Mom and Dad's campground was close by. He and his folks, Uncle Bob and Aunt Julia, were in partnership as concessioners at the East Entrance of the Okefenokee National Wildlife Refuge, which on our side of the swamp, we simply called The Canal. They provided guided boat tours, boat and camping supply rentals, fishing supplies, and snacks and souvenirs under contract with the U.S. Fish and Wildlife Service.

"Why didn't you tell Jar?"

"There was not enough to go on, for one thing. I got in late from work that night and my door was locked just like I left it. When I stepped in, though, things just weren't right. When you live in close quarters like that for a while with everything having to be just so, you know when things are out of place. I would notice it where others would not. Nothing was taken, so Jar would think I was crazy calling him out for so little. Maybe it *is* my imagination.

"Most of all, I didn't want to spoil the reunion or the trip for Jar. He's so protective of his county and kin, he would drop everything to check it out and fix it. I was lucky to get the permit for overnight stays and wanted just the four of us to get away for a couple of nights, though I guess it will be six of us now since Mom asked us to take Ty and Byron. It may be an unusual trip with their inexperience. I just want everything to be right and all of us to have some fun."

March and April were peak periods for overnight canoe trips in the swamp and every available reservation was usually taken within fifteen minutes after the phone line opened in the morning. Chase had to call like everyone else no earlier than two months to the day in advance of our departure date, which would be Monday. More times than not, we had to settle for a day trip.

"Chase, I can understand your thinking, but I don't think it's your imagination. Hamp and I were followed from Athens to Tifton this morning before we shook them. Also, Jar just had a run-in with the FBI agent who was checking on the same people tailing us."

Chase lowered his head and murmured, "Oh, shit." I could tell that he knew something that would shed some light on the mystery.

While he stood there letting the news soak in, I got the envelope with the photos and picked up Hamp's tag numbers on the console. Chase was a worrier and worse than Jar about wanting things right and I could tell all that was going on was taking a heavy toll on what he thought should be the natural order of things.

"Let's go on in," I said. "We need to gather forces for this one."

Chapter 4

Had Jimmy Chase Stone been the girl his mom wanted, he would have been named Precious Gem Stone. Thank goodness the "Jim" part of his name never took and he was always called Chase, after Chase Prairie where early hunters chased down deer that would come out on that space to feed on grass and water plants.

Of all the Stones, I considered Chase the most independent, yet free-hearted. He seldom asked for help, yet he gave of himself without question. He chose to live alone in his camper rather than with Uncle Bob and Aunt Julia, and he faithfully paid rent on the space for it unless he helped Dad with some project on the grounds and, even so, would reluctantly accept a rent reduction of, at most, half of what it should have been. His help was welcomed by Dad, who at fifty was still healthy and strong, but there was a lot to do at Stone's Throw year round. They even enjoyed each other's company.

Chase accepted a good meal twice a week from my folks, who lived in a circa 1960 brick hip-roofed ranch-styled house adjoining the campground, but later repaid them with meat and vegetables from Foodway in town.

He did far more than his share running the concessions at the canal and could easily do it alone, including the snack bar if it came to it, on rainy or cold days when the boat tour service was closed. Everyone with the Wildlife Service including the volunteers liked him and they enjoyed hanging out with him on breaks. He would even deliver a free live tour of the exhibits in their building on request if he were covered for in the concessions complex. His was much more comprehensive and interesting than the spiel gotten from pushing buttons or touching screens. Our family was easing into the swamp area around 1850 as General Floyd was running the Seminoles out, so our knowledge of life in the area was passed down by our ancestors. Chase had considered work with the National Wildlife Service after college, but I'm sure his independence would have been compromised and his camera safaris, hikes and canoe trips would have suffered. He enjoyed the flexibility the family concessions venture offered, and he was near the swamp and family he loved.

He was a worrier by nature and had in his mind how things should be. If something was not in proper alignment or in the correct firing order or not jibing with the natural peaceful order that his mental set of blue prints and specifications called for, it was up to him to make it right. In construction talk, his bubble had to be between the lines.

His freedom and self-reliance had its limits though, and my younger niece, Jan, tried to keep me up to date with his exploits with the ladies. There were so many, they were hard to keep up with unless she happened to talk to the right person in her circle of unmarried girlfriends for the latest. Old news was soon forgotten and overshadowed by the current brow-raiser and no individual could keep score alone. Apparently, Chase was free to give of himself generously along these affable lines and did so, finding time between his work, hobbies, and favors to friends and family. His "rocking good looks" as Jan described him and his inherent desire to do things right kept him in demand. I hoped he got enjoyment from the playful pastime as compensation for his selfless good deeds. Reports on frequency from my niece and other sources suggested that he was in the black and I was glad.

The day was hot for early April and if it was a weekday, the air conditioning in the roomy courthouse would be going full steam. On weekends it was off to save money. We stepped into the stuffiness, locked the glass door with Jar's key and made our way to his office. While we walked, I briefly told Chase how Jar overpowered Gus Bunner after catching him skulking around outside the door and how an apparently long-standing feud was even more galvanized with the encounter. Chase just knitted his brow and frowned.

After Chase and Hamp embraced we all settled into chairs around Jar's metal desk. I gave Hamp the slip of paper with the tag numbers and he handed it to Jar.

"I'll check and see who they are registered to," Jar said. "I'd bet that it's the same outfit that visited your house this morning."

I opened the manila envelopment and took the top three matte-finished photos and gave one each to Jar, Hamp and Chase. "First, you need to check these out. In addition to faultless developing, the pose, light and shadows are award winning. Mine is being framed at Michaels."

They were pictures of Chase's butt.

"Noble! What the hell…that wasn't supposed to be developed, much less enlarged!" Chase looked incredulously at the white two-part orb, his face crimson.

Jar and Hamp were howling. It was a classic moon shot. Chase was bent over, pants down, peering around one side with the comical grin he could give in such moments. It wasn't the first time he had mooned us but it was the first time it was captured on film.

"That's the cutest hairy ass I've seen in a long while," Jar said admiringly. "I'm framing mine too."

Hamp had his held at arm's length, as if admiring a work of art. "This is living room quality. Mine's going next to the bookcase. They'll flip over this at the party tonight."

Chase grabbed for the photo, but he was too slow. "Come on, fellas, hand them over. We've all had our little joke."

"We'll have to see how you conduct yourself this weekend, old buddy," I said. "You should choose your subject better for the last shot on the roll."

Chase just sat there with a concerned look. I guessed he was imagining each person's reaction that would see the photo. "No, from now on, it's Foto Mart for all my developing needs. You guys are assholes."

We had another good laugh and he finally managed a chuckle.

Jar and Hamp put their copy out of Chase's reach. A muffled alarm sounded nearby and less than a minute later, the sounds of siren and horn heralded the city's fire truck headed for a call and they soon faded in the distance. Jar had police and rescue monitors on low volume behind his chair but didn't react to any exchanges that were broadcast. He was officially on vacation for the next seven days.

I finally removed the other pictures from the envelope while they looked on. It was time to address the situation, real and imagined, that Hamp and I found ourselves in, and the one that Chase had been in for weeks and to determine the connection, if any. We were together as we were every year to enjoy ourselves and honor family tics and tradition but felt we were about to address events that could threaten all that. Time to face up.

Chase took the prints and he started separating them into two stacks. One had close-ups of swamp life or scenes of the familiar landscapes, some of them very good. The smaller pile had shots of a white plane in flight over the swamp. Chase spoke as he did this.

"Six weeks ago, I was at the observation tower after lunch taking telephoto shots with plans to send the best ones to sports and wildlife magazines. Some pay pretty well for the ones they can use in their publications, plus I would gain recognition from other editors. I had set up my 300-millimeter Nikon and tripod on the north side of the tower and was looking for photo ops when I noticed to my left a small plane flying low over the swamp headed north. I swung the camera around and tracked its path for a while and, just for the heck of it, snapped a couple of pictures. It went by so fast, I couldn't make out much detail looking through the viewfinder and swinging the camera around, but these two shots made with a fast shutter speed show a couple of fuzzy numbers on the fuselage and the open passenger door, which seemed unusual to me. It's so blurry, it would even be hard to tell the make of the plane."

Chase handed the two pictures to Hamp, who was closest.

"Cessna 182. I've been in one. The door on this one's changed to hinge on top—must be a diver plane. I wonder why it's open." Hamp passed them on to me and, after looking, I gave them to Jar, who took out a magnifying glass and studied the shapes.

"At the time," Chase continued, "I didn't think much about it. The plane flew out of sight and returned within five minutes and left the way it came. There's not a lot of air traffic over the swamp and the sudden appearance of a low flying plane made me curious.

"I guess it was a week or two later I was having lunch at Coffee Bay Shelter on the canal and saw the same plane again heading north, the same direction as before, but this time toward me. When it got to what looked like the south end of Bugaboo Island, it veered to the northwest and out of sight. A few minutes later it reappeared and picked up its earlier route below the island and left."

Jar moved to a large county map on the wall and pointed to it. "You first saw it around here?" He pointed to the left of the tower location.

"Yeah." Chase walked over and traced a path with his finger northward, skirting the south end of Bugaboo Island, and made a counter-clockwise loop and reconnected the imaginary line back at the first sighting point.

"I didn't get a shot of it the second time because of the trees around the shelter. The following Monday about ten in the morning, I took these from a boat where the canal and Canal Run meet." He passed two photos to me. "They show the ID numbers on the fuselage, but it was starting the bank to the northwest like before, so the pilot can't be seen. Even at that low altitude, he probably couldn't be identified anyway. The door was open like in the first pictures."

"What's that below the plane?" Hamp asked.

"Where?" Chase leaned over and picked up the magnifying glass.

"There," Hamp said, pointing. "I don't think it's a bird."

"It's hard to say, but it's two things and neither are wings."

The phone rang and Jar answered, "Mason Jarrett." He started grinning.

"Yes, ma'am, they're here. I've been trying to get them to head on, but they keep hanging around." He listened a moment. "Yes, ma'am. They are loaded on the truck and he's here gabbing too. Want to talk to them?" He smiled at the reply. "In person…I got it. They'll be there directly."

Jar smiled with satisfaction as he cradled the phone, but the smile faded when he saw our glares. "What?"

"You might as well get your butt in that cruiser and come with us," I said. We're not moving chairs around without the one that ratted on us helping too."

"Hey, I've got an image to protect. You two will leave next week, but I'll still be here under fire from your mom. Sheriffs can't be subjected to that."

"What about me?" Chase asked. "I live right under her nose. She won't forget this. Noble, think of something." All our complaints were good-natured but we still had to face Mom.

It was only three o'clock, but Mom knew we should have been there two hours ago. Her punishment for children our age came in the form of mental abuse, and we would be guilt burdened for days after one of her stares. Hamp and I called it "The Look." Dad accepted most of our behavior as part of the male agenda and because of that he even suffered her harsh treatment along with us on occasion. The old adage was correct: "If Momma ain't happy, ain't nobody happy."

"You know the drill," Jar said. "After the greeting and a little small talk, you all three stand around underfoot in her kitchen and she'll have you out of the house within ten minutes. It works every time."

"What about our discussion?" Chase asked. "This is eating me alive—especially after learning Noble and Hamp were followed down here. I've got to talk about it and we need to get it resolved."

"We'll do that," Jar said patiently. At this point, discussing it is all we can do until we can make some sense of it, or something else develops. Try not to let it get to you. I don't see a personal threat yet that justifies action."

Chase and I exchanged glances. People were snooping around at home, breaking into his camper and following Hamp and me to Folkston and I could speak for all of us that we were starting to take it damn personally. I said nothing, though.

"I've got a few calls to make," Jar continued, "so I'll be at Stone's Throw around four. We'll have time to talk some more before dark since the party won't get going before then."

"What're chances of getting those pictures of me, guys?" Chase tried the diplomatic approach. He was a scrapper, but he knew he couldn't whip us all.

Hamp laid down the rules. "If we see the first hint of a bulge in your pants from now until tomorrow night, everyone sees your ass, starting with Momma Dessie. You've got to learn that family reunions are not the place to pick up chicks or get hard-ons."

"Can you say *step-sister*?" Chase asked. Callie is our cousin's stepsister and she's not kin. You guys are ones to talk, following us around last year with your tongues hanging out and brakes smoking. If she had said to you what she said to me, you'd pump in ballast too."

"What in the hell did she say?" Jar asked eagerly with Hamp's and my nodded approval. We may have had our tongues out slightly, and my loins, possibly theirs also, stirred.

"She said I was handsome and cute and she heard I was the best lover and had the biggest dick of all the Stones or Wormants, and she wanted to see how I had remodeled my Airstream."

Hamp and I had Chase on the floor in two seconds, and in another ten, Jar had Chase's pants down and was autographing his right cheek with a Magic Marker. Jar then sat on him while Hamp and I endorsed his left cheek. The howls of protest gave way to gasps for breath that Jar let him take occasionally.

After the struggle, we were all winded and Chase didn't retaliate. After twisting around to check our penmanship, he shook his head in disbelief and calmly pulled up his underwear and Levi's. His golden brown eyes made no contact with ours, but a half smile curled on his lips.

"I guess you guys will check your sleeping bags Monday night before sacking out, but I've got two days to think of something else to get even. Providing the camping equipment and food gives a good supply of possibilities."

Knowing Chase, he would easily out-do us.

* * * *

Driving on South Georgia Parkway around Waycross and Okefenokee Parkway below Folkston was like traveling through a tall endless stockade of vertical pine logs. Tree farms prevailed in this country and the plentiful crops stood in rigid formation on both sides of the highway until their turn came to travel it in the form of long tapers on whining eighteen-wheelers to mills all over South Georgia. Every mile or so, timber parcels were divided according to tree plantings or ownership by single lane dirt access roads that punctuated the endless pattern that the parkway channeled through. Metal gates beyond the right-of-way helped keep the public out and forest fires down. Plowed fire breaks at the edge of the trees also helped keep fires from spreading from carelessly thrown cigarettes onto the grassy highway shoulder.

Chase wanted to drive my, or rather Hamp's, Range Rover to Mom and Dad's, so I got to drive the pea-green '76 pickup with the load of rattling folding chairs and no air conditioning other than the gaping hole in the floorboard. As a reward for my hardship, I stopped at Flash Foods for a thirty-two ounce Mountain Dew Code Red and was a mile behind Hamp and Chase when I resumed the four-mile trip. The road was mostly straight and flat and they were in sight the whole time. After two miles, a gray Dodge pickup pulled from a logging road onto the highway halfway between us. It followed Hamp and Chase the rest of the way to Stone's Throw and turned into the entrance behind them.

I backed Dad's truck next to the pavilion and walked over to Hamp's demonstration of the Rover's bells and whistles. He was raising its ground clearance with the touch of a button to the awe of Chase and Alex Slage, my second cousin and driver of the gray pickup. I shook hands with Alex, since he wasn't into hugged greetings.

"Thought I'd swing by and see if y'all needed help getting set up." He spoke quietly but with purpose and without looking directly at us, cocked his head as if seeking our verbal understanding or approval. "I missed out helping last year because of my other job, but I took off this weekend."

We didn't see any need to respond but I felt he was anxious to open lines of communication that involved questions on his part. "The more the merrier," I finally said. I was starting to feel uncomfortable for some reason but felt obligated to speak since my folks were hosting the weekend.

If he stood straight Alex would be at least 6'3", but his weight was probably less than Chase's 160 pounds. His dark wavy hair was overdue for cutting and made his head look too large for his thin neck. A prominent brow and high, fleshless cheekbones made his dark eyes even darker. His upper lip protruded slightly and was thicker than the lower but a strong square chin kept him from looking wimpy.

Alex worked weekends for an outfitter near Crooked River State Park at St. Marys near the coast and four ten-hour days at Suwannee Canal with Chase and his parents, Uncle Bob and Aunt Julia. Monday was his only day off. He lived on the St. Marys River between Folkston and the town of St. Marys with his dad, my first cousin, who was wheelchair-bound due to a bad auto accident. Alex's stepmother was killed in the wreck. She had a son, Tucker, by a previous marriage. He was Alex's older stepbrother and lived in Atlanta.

By all rights, Alex should have been closer to Chase than anyone because of age and working together and going to the same college, but that was not the case. Chase was four years younger than Hamp and me, but the three of us were close enough to "run the river" together, as western writer Louis L'amour put it. Alex, although he tried not to, always seemed distant to all three of us. He ran around with us when we were younger but he had trouble loosening up and it didn't get any better after college. His stepbrother was even worse and never hung out with us when he went home. Some folks were just harder to get to know, I guessed.

After Hamp showed off the GPS feature in the dash of the Rover, we headed up to the house and stormed into the kitchen like a mob of looters. Mom issued hugs and kisses to us all and we were out of there in seven minutes. I knew because I timed it. We waved at Dad on the way back out as he bush-hogged the pasture that would be Sunday's ball field. There would be plenty of time to catch up on major news with him later.

We all pitched in and swept the concrete walks and floors and started arranging chairs. Mom and Dad had plenty of chairs in a storage room nearby, but we used the funeral home chairs because they had a padded seat. We placed some around the fire pit for that evening's party and the rest under the huge open shelter where the four-note singing would be on Sunday. We purposely left some out of alignment hoping that Mom would only have us change those rather than the whole arrangement.

As we worked, Alex asked Chase about the pictures I developed.

"I'm going to send off four, and possibly a fifth one to magazines," Chase replied. "The rest are so-so."

"Didn't you take some of a plane several weeks ago?"

"Yeah, but they didn't turn out. The speed of the plane and the wind on the tower just caused a blur. I'm sure there's nothing to it—just some guy hot-dogging."

He walked over to the Rover. Hamp had gone up to the house to get cold drinks and I was physically checking the placement of a chair with my feet propped on the seat of a picnic table. The last swallows of my Mountain Dew were warm, and I was wishing Hamp a speedy return.

Chase came back with a stack of prints and put them on the table. "These first five are possibilities for extra cash. If a magazine buys any, they either use them right away or put them in their library for future issues. After some paper work, a check usually comes within sixty days. Last year, I donated a couple of shots to the Refuge Reporter, but I don't think they published them yet."

"These are great," Alex said as he looked through them. "I see what you mean about the plane. These two don't show anything. Are they the only ones?"

"Yeah. The other sighting was from Coffee Bay Shelter, and there were too many trees for a clear shot. Looks like the mystery goes unsolved. I've got other things to worry about, but I still think he could show off for more people closer to a town. Also, access would be easier in case he crashed."

Chase made a show of putting the two unclear plane photos in a nearby trash can. He gathered the others and tapped them on the table to even them up and returned them to the car for safekeeping. The contribution of the partial group of prints to the mystery information bank had lost some punch in the translation to Alex.

I forced myself to get up and check the public showers and restrooms for soap, paper towels and toilet paper and when I finished, Hamp had returned with a recycled milk jug full of sweet tea, blue plastic sixteen ounce cups, and a small cooler with ice. "Save the cups," he said. "Miss Dorothy wants to wash and reuse them." I measured out the ice while he poured. We fixed an extra tea while we were at it because Jar pulled up in his shiny black unmarked cruiser.

"Those chairs over there need straightening," he said, nodding to the baited misaligned row. "Aunt Dottie will surely call you on that."

We just drank our tea. It was possible our little plan would work.

After a while, Alex left to run errands and change for the party. He would be back around dark. The sun was already casting long shadows and daytime noises seemed to be winding down.

Jar slowly poured the last of the tea evenly in our cups and I took the gesture as a way to gain our attention. Hamp and Chase also waited for him to speak.

"Hamp, the cars that followed you and Noble down here are registered to Safepoint Security." Jar pulled a bag of peanut M&M's from his shirt pocket, fished out a couple of nuggets and popped them in with practiced ease. They crunched loudly before meeting their fate.

"They were the ones snooping around at home according to Freddie," I said.

Jar continued. "Their home office is in Atlanta and they have branches in many towns in the southeast. Most addresses are postal box numbers, but some are offices in larger towns and cities. Their biggest business is providing security guards for companies and individuals but they do surveillance work in fraud and divorce cases also. If you think about it, outfits like that can be places and do things that the ordinary citizen can't, plus they carry guns. I've read of operations like that being traced to some shady characters. The balance between legal and illegal tends to favor badges, ID's and permits, so it would be a perfect front to cover suspicious activity. The way those people have behaved today, I'd have to think real negative of them. Another reason to think that way is that the plane is registered to a man who has a charter service called Southpoint Flights down in Key West, and the phone number for the local Safepoint Security is also in his name."

Out of the corner of my eye, I noticed Chase slump slightly.

Chapter 5

It was only six in the evening and people wouldn't start wandering in for the party until around eight when it was almost dark. Mom made a snap inspection and, sure enough, had us straighten the wayward chairs. We never understood what difference it would make since she never came around during the Saturday party. She just had to be in control I reckoned.

We sat in the covered pavilion near the edge in a half-circle watching a family of semi-domesticated mallard ducks foraging for food in the shallows of the fishing pond. Years ago they stopped by Stone's Throw and decided it was far enough south to go for the winter. Rather than pack up and leave the following spring, they homesteaded, convinced it would be foolish to leave the abundant wild food and tidbits provided by campers for a more uncertain life. They were so far out of wild that their atrophied wings could only give flight to their large bodies for fifty feet, tops. A chicken could fly as far.

We digested the information Jar had just provided. It confirmed what I guessed we already knew but didn't want to know—the mysterious plane had a connection to the people following us and snooping around our home in Athens. I was also sure the break-in of Chase's camper was connected.

"Well, it's obvious the plane was not meant to be seen by me," Chase said, "and especially not photographed. Now you guys are involved with your knowledge of the sightings and photos. This is not going to blow away, is it?"

"I don't think throwing Alex off the scent will be the end of it, if that's what you mean," I said. All three jerked their heads toward me. Chase lowered his in defeat as if he had broken a rule or missed a shot.

Jar returned his gaze to the pond and folded his arms over his massive chest. "Keep talking, Noble."

"Chase, you need to do the talking," I said. "Most of my thoughts are conjecture. I do know that you didn't show Alex all the photos, and the only reasons to do that would be to make him think you had nothing on the plane and to convince him you had lost interest in the whole thing. Do you think he's connected with the security company in some way?"

"I don't know what to think. I told three people about the plane after the second sighting—your mom and dad one night at supper and Alex at work. I don't think I mentioned taking pictures to Uncle Hank and Aunt Dottie, but I did to Alex. Since then he's shown a lot of concern over additional plane sightings and development of the pictures I took. Unless he or your folks told someone that might have interest in my activities, I can't help but think he has more than a casual interest in them. By not showing him the good plane pictures I thought I could put the situation on hold a while until we four talked about it and tried to figure out what's going on. Right now my thoughts won't keep Alex out and it worries me that he's into something he shouldn't be."

"Do you suspect he had anything to do with Wednesday night?" I asked.

Chase gave me a perturbed look but we both knew it would have to come up sooner or later. We needed to get everything out in the open right away.

"What happened Wednesday night?" Hamp asked. Jar sat patiently with his arms still folded.

"I think my camper was searched that night. Nothing was missing, but several things were out of place and I could tell my mattress had been lifted. The door hadn't been jimmied and was locked the way I left it, so whoever it was could pick locks or had access to a key and didn't want me to know they had been inside. Mom and Dad have a key on their ring of work keys and so does Uncle Hank, but I asked and it wasn't any of them.

"I feel guilty thinking Alex had anything to do with it, but he knew I was working late that night and he thought I was expecting to receive the developed pictures in the mail by then. Noble and I later decided he would bring them when he came down to save the cost of mailing them, but I didn't tell Alex about that until he asked about them at work Thursday."

"Did you know he followed you part of the way from town a while ago?" I asked.

"Yeah. I saw him pull out of the logging road in the mirror. Yesterday, I told him you were hoping to come in the Range Rover, so he must have figured it was you and Hamp."

I avoided Hamp's stare. It was going to be harder to trick him into taking the Rover the next time we went down but I would think of something.

Jar stretched his legs out and crossed them at his ankles. "You guys think Alex knows about Hamp delaying the Safepoint cars in Tifton?"

"If he's in cahoots with them, he does," I answered, "but I don't think he learned about it until after we met at your office. Otherwise, he would have intercepted us there to monitor our arrival and find out if we knew anything. I don't know about you guys, but I sense a feeling of urgency on his part. Now he knows we stopped in town because Chase drove here with Hamp. He may not know that we met with Jar but if he's part of the puzzle he knows all that surveillance has a hole in it from Tifton to this side of Folkston and it would surely concern him that we had contacts he was not aware of. If we had something solid, we could have given it to Gus Bunner in Jar's office instead of a knot on the forehead."

"Fellas, aren't we making too big a deal out of this?" Hamp asked. "Sure, we met in town and saw some pictures and discussed them but I don't think we've seen or heard enough to keep condemning Alex."

"Have you forgotten we were followed down here?" I asked. "The closest connection we have to that are the pictures I developed of a plane that is, in turn, connected to the security company. Information on us had to come from down here and Alex had it."

"It still seems awfully weak to me. I could better understand some corporate spies keeping an eye on me as a competitor's lawyer, but none of my law work so far has been that covert. I doubt you have many secrets in your construction work either. We need something more concrete. I can tell it's just a matter of minutes before your imagination conjures up some elaborate explanation of this whole thing and Alex is not here to defend himself."

The points Hamp made were well made. When he got wound up he could come up with some good arguments. He was also right that I had it all figured out. "I do happen to have a good theory, but I'll wait and see what the professional comes up with." I glanced at Jar.

"I think we all know where this could go," he said, "but we need to lay everything out first—Chase, do you have any more bombshells to drop? You should have told me about your intruder."

"I know, but let's don't allow any of this to spoil the weekend or the swamp trip. I'm starting to agree with Hamp that we need something better to go on and I've told everything I know."

"We won't change our plans over any of this but we should all be aware of what we might be up against. Two or three more days of normal activity shouldn't change things much. So far, I don't see anything that we can take action toward, but I'll throw one more thing in and see if it catches light: The more I looked at those blurs under the plane with magnification, the more they looked like a duffel bag suspended by a parachute."

* * * *

The public rest rooms were at the far end of the shelter and we took a break after drinking all the iced tea. Jar's remark about the duffel "caught light" for me and I was ready to share the drama unfolding in my mind. We returned to our seats and I started with my theory without preamble.

"Drugs are being delivered, probably from South or Central America, to the Keys and put on a small, apparently legitimate charter plane. It flies up the east coast, cuts across sparsely populated South Georgia farmland and low country and the package is dropped on a remote end of a nearly inaccessible island in a wilderness. A shallow draft boat or canoe is used to pick up the goods, transport it to Steven Foster State Park to avoid refuge security at the canal, and a short hop to I-75 puts it on a major artery headed to dealers all over the Southeast or farther. If no traffic laws were broken, no one would suspect a fisherman or canoeist enough to stop him. It would be clear sailing to drop-off points where those particular risks would have to be examined and compensated for by another set of people.

"Our main concern right now is that we know about the exchange point but we don't know the consequences of such knowledge—will they change their method of operation, or will they press the issue with us in some way?"

I used that last statement to rile them up a little and break them out of the spell I had them in. "Any body else got the same bingo card?" They started to stir a little.

"Jeez, Noble."

What Hamp really said was, "How do you come up with all that shit? This is sleepy little Folkston, Georgia and you've gone international drug ring on us. It's not anything at all like that and nobody's going to press any issue with us—especially like shooting me in the ass again."

"Are they, Jar?" Hamp added aloud.

"I was thinking drug operation," Jar said, ignoring Hamp's question. "But why the Keys? Why not Miami or another coastal city with better access. Key West is so isolated."

"That's the whole point," I replied. "Who would suspect a drug shipment to originate in such an inaccessible place? The way it's set up, every time it touches land it's in a remote area 'til it can blend in with travelers. Naturally they would avoid the main drag out of the Keys because it's well patrolled, but even the road trip from the swamp to the Interstate originates on a back dead end road and passes through secluded farmland."

"What about Alex?" Chase asked me. "I go along with the drug theory but where does he fit in? You left him out completely."

"I did so purposely. Hamp's right—until we get something more solid to go on we need to quit pinning things on him."

"I'm willing to go along with that," Jar said, "but we should keep in mind that someone has to monitor this side of the swamp—especially the Fish and Wildlife people's activities—to avoid encounter with a routine patrol or inspection. They're not always on a rigid schedule." He glanced over at Hamp.

"Hamp, does the drug operation assumption fit in with your thinking or are we on the wrong ball field?"

"Hell, Jar, I was working on a wife-dumping scheme but that stalled out because of the frequency of the flights—unless, of course, she was a big person in a lot of pieces." Sometimes Hamp could get off track if the ruts weren't deep but we smiled, knowing he was just jerking our chain.

Years ago, a man rented a small plane near Athens to take his murdered wife, stuffed in a barrel, on a one way trip to the Okefenokee. He stopped in the middle of the night at a small airport near the swamp to remove the passenger door so he could push the barrel out in flight. The unusual late night activity at the airport led a local citizen to call the law and the guy was caught with his cargo. No doubt Hamp's thinking was tainted by that true story and by his belief that Charlton County would never be a drop-off for drugs.

"How often was it, Chase—once a week the plane came around? That's a lot of drugs if you think about it." Hamp had started to come around to our thinking.

Chase nodded. "Every time on a Monday that I know of. It's a slow day for all of us visitor-wise, but tiresome for the refuge workers facing maintenance and house- and grounds-keeping problems from a busy weekend. Paper work is heavy too."

Some of the camping Stones were returning from the canal and from visits with family while others were just arriving and setting up, so we decided to break up the meeting. We certainly didn't want to interfere with their chores. Jar looked at his watch and stretched. "I need to go and get cleaned up, fellas. I'll be back before eight." He folded the top of his bag of reprieved M&M's and put them in his shirt pocket for later.

Hamp and I headed up to the house to shower, change and bond with my folks, and Chase made his way to the camper. As we passed the trash can, I threw in my cup but caught myself when Hamp cleared his throat. I reached in to retrieve it and noticed the two bad photos of the plane were gone.

With a lot of discipline, we would all try to have a good time at the party despite the dark shadows of the unknown hanging over us.

*   *   *   *

Soon after I was able to dress by myself my sense of style became dulled, and if it weren't for Jar's guidance and Hamp's sympathy and hand-me-downs, a lot of doors would be closed to me. Bonnie helped with her input when we went out and would arrive early to pick me up and make the clothing selections. I was usually safe selecting my boxers and would meet her at the door so attired to save time by dressing only once.

For the belly-rub that night, Hamp and I, under his direction, wore our Kahala "Aloha" shirts—his was navy and olive with palm trees and mine was tan and sage with big flowers. Hamp got them last year on vacation when he and Sally went to Hawaii. We both wore cotton canvas cargo shorts by Sportif in a color that, I was told, went well with the shirts. Sebago "Docksides" for me and Sperry Top-Siders for Hamp, no socks, were the footwear.

Chase showed up in Supplex river shorts, a dark blue camp shirt with Hawaiian print, and leather sandals. Jar switched to a white Duckhead polo shirt with the emblem on the chest, but the khakis and boat shoes didn't change.

We all cut a striking figure even if it was just for family. Who knew? Maybe somebody's eligible friend would be at the party or a technicality present itself like it did for Chase last year. There was a whole forest beyond the family tree.

* * * *

It looked liked the perfect place for a witches' coven. Old time traffic smudge pots filled with citronella oil dotted the perimeter of the bonfire area. They came from an era before battery operated flashing lights and I often wondered what happened to the millions of smelly, smoky caution lamps no longer used by highway departments. Dad only had ten.

After a meal of hamburgers, hot dogs, Mom's potato salad and baked beans, we left the shelter lights with the job of attracting insects and gathered in the open air around the fire pit. A lazy breeze blew the smoke across the pond and interfered with the flight pattern of weaker bugs headed our way.

Jimmy Buffet CD's, along with the iced-down beer and white wine, helped get us in the right frame of mind, and then cousins Tommy Hasty, "Flint" Stone and Owen Lee took up their guitar, fiddle and harmonica, respectively, and expertly delivered traditional shit-kicking music balanced with that of currently popular artists like my favorite, Dave Matthews. Many of us knew the words to a lot of his songs and nobody seemed to mind that Chase and I were off key (we liked to think we were harmonizing when we had had a few).

Of all people, Jar was the singer in the family. He sang a couple of solos and Hamp joined in with him on a few more. Much applause from forty-some-odd revelers followed their numbers.

All but three of the young ladies to show up were kin. One was Alex's date—a tallish redhead named Charlene with low-riding flares and high-riding halter-top. Platform sandals and ample bosom made her look a bit top-heavy but she would have never hit the ground the way she was clinging to Alex. I understood why they left before anyone else. They were hardly missed anyway since they stayed mostly to themselves. I would never have matched them as a couple but was glad for Alex that the rest of the night looked promising for him.

The other two un-kin girls were teenage schoolmates of local cousins and a bit plain even for a young male Stone's unrefined tastes, but the teen boys still showed off for them and were rewarded by giggles and whispers. It was enough to make you sick.

If Momma Dessie had seen her precious Stones around one o'clock Sunday morning she would have sworn we were all switched at birth. The younger ones had reluctantly honored their curfews, so that gave the more mature ones an opportunity to show off their tattoos and piercings (other than ears) much to Jar's chagrin. Of the fourteen people still partying, eight had one or the other or both, and I wondered how that compared with the national average. One male had a ring he wouldn't show in mixed company but he showed it to the guys behind the rest rooms. I decided I would stay with the nipple ring if I could get approval.

Later, Hamp and I stepped into the shadows to take a whiz and we returned to find Chase with his pants down showing everybody the damning script on his backside, telling them God knows what. Icy stares, even from some of the men slowed our return. You would have thought we violated the Mona Lisa. We were about to retreat when Jar waved us over to his deputy's cruiser idling in the parking lot. He was sitting in the passenger seat. We gladly hurried over to the safety of law enforcement but my aft hawsehole tightened anyway, and not because of Chase's sympathetic onlookers. Something was up.

* * * *

"Your place got hit a couple of hours ago," Jar said in our direction when we were in hearing range. We stepped up to the open passenger window where his massive face was framed.

"The security guys from this morning?" I asked, not surprised at the news.

"The same. Your neighbor called Marge, my dispatcher, rather than waking up Hank and Dottie. Clement here got the details from her on his cell phone—I'm not carrying mine—and came out to tell us. Your buddy Pope got winged when he shot one of the guys for drawing his gun. Both are in the hospital."

"Freddie shot?" Hamp looked a little pale. "Is he all right?"

"He's the one that called so he must be OK. He told Marge that he didn't let on he knew where you two were on his report so you could finish the trip. He said you could get with the police there for the report when you returned. He's at Athens Regional Medical Center, but I'd wait 'til morning to call him. Marge told Clement he sounded kind of groggy."

Enjoying every minute of it, I thought to myself.

Jar lifted the sheet on the clipboard and the next one was blank. "This it, Clement?"

"Everything Marge told me. I had her repeat it all twice."

"I guess you ought to head back and check on the place, Hamp," I said. "I can ride the bus back after the reunion."

We looked up and saw Chase approaching with a worried, questioning look.

"We may need to think about that some," Hamp said quietly. "I think we're needed more here."

Chapter 6

▼

I called Freddie Pope around eight the next morning. Six hours before, we had given Chase the news of the break-in at our place in Athens, and straightened up a little around the pavilion before heading for bed. Three or four hangers-on had remained around the dying campfire but our beer buzzes had switched off upon getting the news of the break-in and we decided to leave it with them. Our thoughts had turned to the growing mystery and to Freddie's status in the hospital, and the magic was gone. I was fairly sure he would be all right but I wanted to hear it from him.

"Shit, Noble, I'm fine. I took a bullet through the outer thigh and it hurts like hell but they have good stuff around here to take for that. It probably would have hurt worse if he had got me in the vest and the impact knocked me against something. There's a bullet hole in the wainscot you and Hamp just refinished in the hall, but it looks like a knot from a distance."

"Did they go into my darkroom?"

"That's where I challenged them when they finally found it. Being off the kitchen had them confused for a while. They went all over the house looking for it while I crouched in the shadows of the breakfast nook. I gave them time to rummage through your files and boxes to see what they were after, but I guess it was the box of negatives I took home. They were about to leave with a couple of your cameras when I nailed them—guess they hated to leave empty-handed. One of them pulled his gun when I identified myself and yelled for them to stop. I had to shoot him in the stomach and when he reacted he pulled off a shot and got me in the leg. They think he is going to pull through and I sure hope so. He's the first person I ever had to shoot and I'm having a hard time with it. Thank goodness the other guy didn't try anything."

"At least you are OK," I said. "Freddie, I never intended for you to risk your life over this. You should have called for backup."

"Cindy called when she heard the shots and the patrol was there in two minutes. She went home a while ago to get me another pair of pants to go home in and called to tell me my supervisor was giving Channel 2 and 5 an interview in Hamp's yard. It'll be in the papers too, I guess. I'll tape the news and get an extra paper for y'all."

"You guys are going to stay down there, aren't you? I'm thinking you have things to work out there before you come back—at least it sounded like it yesterday. Don't take any chances though. Whoever is behind this must have some incentive."

"I think we'll stay if you don't need us there. Sounds like we won't even have to call the insurance company because I should be able to repair any damage."

"A glass in the back door is all you'll have to work on. The hole in the wall will be fun to show people. I'm going home today and I'll make sure the place is secure until you get back. Cindy said she had already cleaned up the blood in the house but I'll save my bloody pants for y'all to see."

I thanked Freddie for everything and we hung up. Hamp shuffled in a little later, and I made us peanut butter toast to go with our coffee. Mom never made breakfast on reunion day since the stove was tied up cooking for the Big Meal. I told Hamp about the call while we ate on the back porch and he hung on every word, as usual not offering any of his own. He did agree we needed to be fishing down there because that's where they were going to be biting next.

* * * *

Four-note singing was a musical event at our get-togethers ever since I could remember. It emphasized participation, not performance, and the style came from singing schools in the colonial period. It was particularly preserved in the rural South and seemed to have made a major resurgence in cities and campuses throughout the United States in the last decade. It was known by several names, but the most popular were Sacred Harp, fasola, and shape-note singing. The music is printed in patent notes in The Sacred Harp songbook and the shape of the note head indicated the syllables FA, SOL, LA, and MI. Mom always called it four-note singing because her forebears did. The oblong songbook was first published in 1844, but she had copies of the current 1991 Edition.

Singers sat facing inward in a hollow square and that was how we had arranged the chairs the night before. A leader stood in the middle and beat time with the hand to a song he or she selected. There were no musical instruments. Everyone was offered a chance to lead and it was seldom passed up, especially if they had a song they liked to hear. Selections included psalm tunes, fugal tunes, odes and anthems by early composers, and folk songs and revival hymns in the latest songbook were popular with the younger set. Some of the most popular hymns were Rock of Ages, Amazing Grace, and Sweet Rivers.

The Key Stones, as Dad called the singing family, spouses and significant others, started around nine in the morning and tapered off by late afternoon. There was usually breaks in the morning and afternoon when the Stepping Stones do-si-doed to some fiddling by cousin Flint and square dance calls by Uncle Berrian, who could do some mean buck dancing after a couple of whistle-wetting trips to his truck. Everyone who wanted to took their opportunity to sing and lead songs or kick up their heels, including Hamp and Jar. As with both the singing and dancing, the fun was in the participation, but many chose to sit to the side and hear the age-old sounds of voice and fiddle drift over the grounds, losing themselves to another time. Chase and I charitably found other activity and thereby spared anyone the embarrassment of asking us not to sing or dance.

There was plenty else to do and we saw fit to kick butt in a doubles horseshoe game and would be playing the winners of the next game. We had time to top off with Mom's sweet iced tea in the pavilion and did so, taking cupfuls back with us in case there was an air pocket. We took another route back through some thick scrub pines to the shade of the ancient and mossy live oak that easily shaded both horseshoe pits and the forty-foot space between them. It was along this unbeaten path that we spotted Alex's older stepbrother, Tucker, with a blood-soaked shirt held to his face.

*　*　*　*

Last year, it was a fishing hook in young nephew Ernie's ear. The year before, a line drive popped Sam Cooder, cousin and softball shortstop-turned-right-fielder, in the nuts. Many prior reunions were referred to by the most outstanding misfortune such as the year the yellow jacket stung little Noble on the bottom lip or the year teenager Noble broke a big toe when he dropped the cooler on it. There were six such years with my name tacked to them, two of them from adulthood. The good far outweighed the bad at our gatherings but the disasters, minor and not so minor, made the gatherings much easier to remember, gruesome as it sounded. Judging by the blood, dirt and grass stains, Tucker's condition would be the year's event and it looked serious.

"Tucker, wait up!" I yelled. Charlene Luther, Alex's date—or so I thought, was rushing ahead toward the parking lot with keys in hand and Tucker was close behind. He glanced our way but kept moving.

"Tucker, stop!" Chase called out. He had reached Tucker first and grabbed a shoulder but his hand was knocked away.

"Leave me alone! I'm all right—it's just a nosebleed—leave me alone, OK?" He kept up his pace.

"We need to call an ambulance," Chase said firmly. "There's too much blood."

"I've had them before, Chase," he snapped. "Just make my apologies and say I had an emergency at work if anyone asks. Tell them something so they won't be concerned. I'm getting out of here."

Tucker got into the passenger side of his Mersedes 240SL and Charlene spun it away as if it was hers.

Chase and I stood there a moment trying to make sense of the situation. Tucker's condition was not a result of a softball game or basketball accident because someone would have raised the alarm by now. Then, Alex's girlfriend, or whatever, drives Tucker off in his car, presumably to Atlanta where he lived. I wondered if we should tell someone about it and had an idea Chase wondered the same.

Still without a word, we finally turned and retraced our steps, then headed in the direction Tucker and Charlene came from. Deeper into the pines, we found Alex balled up clutching his stomach and groaning. His left eye was starting to swell and his upper lip was split and bleeding. When he saw us approaching, his lanky limbs slowly unfolded and he started trying to get to his feet like a newborn foal.

"Just leave me alone, OK? I'm just not feeling well and need to rest a minute." It was an effort for Alex to speak.

"We just saw Tucker and can figure out that you were fighting, Alex," I said impatiently. "What the hell is going on?"

I reached out to steady him but he pivoted away and lost his balance. Chase caught him before he fell.

"Goddammit, it's none of your business! We had a misunderstanding and we worked it out so just let it be." It was still an effort for him to speak but he was getting his wind back. He rubbed the back of his hand across the blood that ran to his chin.

"You ought to see a doctor and get stitches on that lip," Chase said. "Might ought to check for broken ribs, too."

Alex's right hand was clutching his side. His face would have turned into a snarl but the swelling masked it. "I'm going home to get cleaned up," he said firmly. "Then, after the dinner, I'll come back and pick up Dad. You can help by bringing him to the parking lot then so nobody will see me if you like, but otherwise you need to mind your own fucking business."

He had never talked that boldly to us but he had never been that hurt or mad around us either. He closed his eyes and seemed to will us away but his legs buckled again and we barely broke his fall as he dropped to the pine straw. He was still conscious but it was obvious he needed to rest.

The few fights that I couldn't get out of that weren't settled after two or three blows exhausted me so, mentally and physically, that all I wanted to do was steal away afterward and lick my wounds. Even professional boxers rested after three minutes and the average Joe couldn't go near that long unless some of that time was spent in flight or time out. Such intense encounters were like being in a low gear at a high RPM—little progress for a lot of output—and Alex and Tucker had apparently revved up their engines.

We decided Alex's lip would get by without stitches, but we were concerned about internal damage. He was such an ass about going to the doctor that we half carried, half dragged his bony frame through the wooded area to Chase's camper and got him inside without being seen. Chase turned up the air conditioner and put ice in a plastic food bag while I got Alex settled on the sofa/bed. By the time I got the drying blood off his face and the ice pack in place he was asleep. He had put up no resistance to our help after his collapse, and his normal aloofness had given way to unreserved vulnerability.

"What now?" Chase asked after removing Alex's shoes. The overhead air conditioning unit almost drowned him out as it struggled with the day's heat.

"Right now, we need to get back before we're missed. We definitely shouldn't let on any of this happened or it will screw up the picnic. If it gets out later then so be it. Hopefully, it's just sibling rivalry or a quarrel over something and they have already worked it out. I don't see anything else cropping up with Tucker if he's going back to Atlanta, and Alex apparently doesn't want our help, so let's just leave him alone. I'm not even sure what we'd do for him anyway with our suspicions of him hanging over us."

Chase jerked his head toward me. "Damn, Noble, we just carried him a hundred yards and made him comfortable out of the heat and you cleaned the blood off his face and hands so we are not exactly throwing him away. We'll do what needs to be done and you know it. He's family."

Chase was right, and I felt bad about what I said. We had decided the day before that we didn't have anything strong against Alex, and I saw no connection between his altercation with his stepbrother and the mysterious airplane visits to the swamp. For the time being, we needed to put things back on hold and wait for the next move, which may or may not be ours to make. We could easily get Alex to the parking lot later in the afternoon and help his dad roll his wheelchair there to be driven home. No one would be the wiser.

We left the camper quietly and headed back to the horseshoe games. Chase was quiet and I could tell the situation between Alex and Tucker had unsettled him. He liked for things to be on an even keel, especially when family was concerned. When he finally spoke again, it was on a lighter note than I expected and I was glad.

"If all that was over Charlene, I think they should raise their standards a good bit. Anybody willing to shed blood over that camp follower needs to check out the other talent a little better."

I started to tell Chase about Hamp and me willing to fight to the death over Lainey Delbeck when we were seventeen, but thought better of it. Chase was slow to judge but he would have been critical of our behavior if I had described Lainey's lack of radiance. Had the radiant camp follower been around back then, we would have been done with her before we got our pants down. As they say: that was then, this is now.

* * * *

Cousins Ty and Byron Slappey didn't arrive until after two o'clock and it was a grand entrance. If we were able to keep the Alex/Tucker fight from everyone, the reunion would be known as the one when Ty and Byron's '98 Chrysler Sebring caught fire in the parking lot soon after they arrived and melted Dad's new ninety-seven dollar state-of-the-art poly wheelbarrow that was parked nearby. Luckily, Byron was able to sling their luggage from the trunk and stomp out one of Ty's smoldering tennis shoes before it was a complete loss.

In spite of the somehow humorous event, the Stone Family convention that year was rated "best ever" by the rating committee, which included all those attending. Chase and I had to rate it a step down to "outstanding" because of the fight, but that was still good. We had hoped no one would find out about the scuffle. The burning yellow Sebring was missed by no one, however, and affected the ratings in a positive way, especially when the nearly empty gas tank exploded. Uncle Whet got it all on his new video camera and probably a thousand pictures were taken of the show at varying stages of incineration.

In addition to the pyric display, the best singing was sung, the best dances were stepped, the biggest fish was angled and the best food was tasted. The last ten percent of the day was always devoted to those ponderings while empty bowls and coolers were gathered, lost shoes and shirts hunted, and tired, smelly, whiny kids were paraded about for a last hug and kiss from those whose age entitled them to do so.

Most of the Georgia and Florida dwellers would leave by six and get home by ten. Those living farther away camped another night and left early Monday morning. Grady Slage, Alex's dad and Tucker's stepfather, was the first to leave at around three because of the pain in his hip. Chase and I shook Alex awake from a sound sleep in the camper, and after a minute or so, stood by while he tried standing. That went well, though I could tell his ribs hurt terribly. Afraid he would fall, I followed the tall lanky figure to the rear of the Airstream where he dampened his long dark hair at the aqua colored lavatory and rearranged his bed-head hair with spread fingers, his knuckles brushing the low curving ceiling of the camper a couple of times as he did so. He took a half step to the left to the small commode and I stepped out while he peed. Chase wrapped the two plates of food that were in the tiny refrigerator. He and I had taken them to Alex at different times, unaware that the other had done the same. The food was declined both times but he would surely be hungry before dark.

The three of us wove our way back through the pines and I cut across to the pavilion and wheeled Cousin Grady to his specially-equipped Aerostar van in the parking lot. It was rigged so he could get in and out and drive it even with his paralysis but I never saw him do it.

Alex was already behind the wheel and stared ahead while I helped Grady to his seat. Sunglasses covered most of the swollen black eye but the split lip would show easily if Alex turned toward the passenger side. He continued to face forward as did Grady when settled in his seat. They didn't speak to each other. Chase folded the wheelchair and put it in back.

"Catch y'all later," I said when the van was started. Grady nodded as the electric window whined up. We stood in silence while they faded into the wavy heat from the highway.

"Alex said 'thanks'," Chase finally said, still looking up the road.

"He did?"

"Made eye contact too."

"That was a major commitment."

"I know."

Chapter 7

We all were at the canal by 7:30 a.m. including Ty and Byron, but there was really no rush. In order to get to Round Top Shelter and set up camp before dark, we didn't have to be in the water until 10:00, so there would be plenty of time for photo-op stops and hanging out in general. The last time we went on that thirty-two mile round trip, we arrived early at Round Top, the first overnight stop, and ended up trying to play cards on the double carport-sized platform in a vast marshy prairie with a half-sized deck that a previous early arriver had made out of scrap cardboard and paper. It was lovingly tied with string and left in the sign-in box.

Uncle Bob, Chase's dad, already had three identical red Old Town Discovery canoes on the launching ramp with three identical piles of camping gear by their side. We entered the concession building with our coolers and found Aunt Julia piling packaged food and drink from the giant stainless steel refrigerator/freezer onto the snack counter.

"It's so good of you boys to take Ty and Byron along on your trip," she said. "I doubt there's much wholesome to do way up there in Memphis, what with all the crime and corruption. At least they're not stuck with those two trollops any more—they were just after the Slappey money and were trying to get it by marrying into it. Good riddance, I say." She still managed a smile.

Divorce was rare in our family but Ty and Byron married a couple of gold-digger sisters who thought owning a used car place in Tennessee was next to printing your own money. The problem was, vehicles that traveled the state's ailing roads and highways took an early trip to the previously owned vehicle vendors when they should have gone directly to the salvage yard. Uncle Graham said the last time he was down that they were improving the roads and joked that the Tennessee category in the Blue Book auto value guide was going to be eliminated.

Chase's Mom was only forty-three but her hair was graying fast and she already wore it in a bun. She was outspoken on many matters and had opinions and solutions ready whether asked for or not, but they were usually offered with a take-it-or-leave-it smile. She and Uncle Bob looked a lot like Grant Wood's portrait of the solemn rural man with wire rim glasses and pitchfork and his bun-haired wife standing in front of a house and barn, but Chase's folks were much more cheerful and upbeat—perhaps a rarity after working with the public for so long. I'd like to get a picture of them some day in the same pose but with their infectious smiles. Their house even looked a lot like the one in the portrait except for the Gothic window upstairs.

Some of the food items such as the rib eyes and baking potatoes were bought earlier by Chase in Folkston and had his hand-written notes on the packages declaring, "Trip stuff—don't touch!" Other items were stock from the snack bar labeled with the same warning and he got those at cost. Chase and Jar began dividing the marked provisions equally into three coolers while Hamp and I returned to the canoes to distribute and lash down the gear after placing the unwettables in plastic trash bags. Afternoon thunderstorms were a good possibility that time of year and could dampen the enjoyment if something critical got wet like a sleeping bag or Jar's snacks. The accompanying lightning was considered by many to be the greatest danger in the swamp—worse than alligators unless they were fed or disturbed—but there was little precaution that could be taken against it other than avoiding trees, which were scarce near the canoe trails anyway.

Uncle Bob was talking to Ty and Byron as we walked up. "I tried to get Alex to wait until you fellas got here and y'all could paddle the canal together," Bob said as he placed a portable toilet at each canoe. "Said he was in a hurry but y'all could do it another time."

Hamp and I froze momentarily, then stood. I took a few steps to look around the concession building and saw the Dodge pickup at the far end of the parking lot.

"He's on the canal now?" I asked in disbelief.

"Yeah—I thought you knew. Said he was going to the Canal Run Shelter and back and might be all day. We fixed him a sandwich and some drinks in a cooler. Otherwise, he would have gone without anything."

"What time did he leave?"

"'Bout ten after. He'll have forty-five minutes on you by the time you get on the water. You'll never catch him with the loads you have."

"What was he going there for?" I had to ask. Alex wasn't all that outdoorsy despite the nature of his two jobs, though he hung with us when we asked him along. After Uncle Grady's car wreck we seemed to drift apart, seeing less and less of him. I was trying to keep my suspicions at bay.

"Enjoying the swamp same as you guys, I guess. He did say something about exercise and building up his arms and shoulders. Say, that was a nasty lick he got playing softball yesterday, wasn't it?"

"Sure was." I wondered how he explained his injuries.

"If y'all run across him, try to talk him into camping with you. He never gets out anymore and something like that would do him good. You have enough to feed an army anyway. Mom and I can handle this place for a couple of days and Sandy will be coming in after school."

We didn't say anything and returned to our work. Hamp had typically said little all morning but I could tell his mind was awhirl with Bob's news. Mine was too and I would help him out with an explanation as soon as I figured out something. My first thought was that it was Monday, and Monday was airplane day. I could build on that and pass it by him when I ironed out a few things.

After several trips, Chase and Jar had the full coolers and dry bags of food ready for us to pack. Ty and Byron helped some but mostly argued about who was going to be on what end of the canoe. Jar had held back a smaller dry bag that I assumed contained some of the no-no food group for quick access.

The trick was to balance and distribute the loads just so. I was glad Ty and Byron didn't get involved in that part of the packing, because I had it down to a science. I even liked to lash everything down but the cooler lids, though we certainly wouldn't be careless enough to capsize in alligator territory even if they were seldom aggressive. Also, it would be next to impossible to lose equipment in the still water, especially since most trails, other than the lakes and canal, are barely deep enough to float a canoe. It was often hard to take deep effective strokes in many places because of the vegetation and submerged peat along the narrow trails.

My precautions were probably a carry-over from white water canoeing on the Upper Chattahoochee and Etowah Rivers. Fool me twice, shame on me. Anyway, we might as well have used some of the rope Chase always insisted on taking.

*   *   *   *

Byron fell out of the canoe before we even left the launching ramp and they tipped enough to take on a couple gallons of water. His arms churned the silky amber water to a yellow froth and his loud harsh cry caused an older couple sitting on an outside bench to seek safety inside the concession building and watch through the glass doors. The curses and cries for help ran together in a way that neither was clear and I doubted the couple understood a word of the tirade other than several fairly well-pronounced "Alligator!" screams by Ty. The more Byron thrashed about, the farther he got from shore and he was in waist deep water before he realized he could stand on the submerged concrete boat ramp. By then he was completely soaked. Aunt Julia, wringing her hands in her apron, came rushing out after hearing the clamor and seeing the fear in the older couple's eyes. She stared in smiling wonder at the commotion. She was disappointed when she realized it was not tourist generated, but caused by a sinking Stone and she began issuing orders to the rest of us to help him before somebody we knew came along. Jar, Hamp, Chase and I continued to stare in disbelief as Ty's slight frame fell in the murky water while trying to reach his paddle that he dropped during the original melee. His screams got even worse. Uncle Bob was no longer in the area but I heard his distinguishable laugh, this one a deep disabling laugh, around the corner of the building. I could tell that Chase was trying to make eye contact with the rest of us because he knew his devil-inspired grin would break us up too. We didn't fall for it.

By 8:30, we had the water bailed out of the Slappey canoe and were ready to go again. Ty and Byron didn't bother to change because they were drying out quickly in the morning sun and heat. After trying to assure them again that the alligators wouldn't bother them, they gave in and we were on our way.

On trips like that, I always had fleeting second thoughts as we made the first few strokes to pull out of the inertia influenced by our personal 360 pounds and 150 pounds more or less of gear and food. I also always looked back to see if we untied the painter. Hamp always looked back to see if I was paddling. Once we got going it wasn't so bad, but it would be paddling every inch of the way and our backs, shoulders and arms would be under fiery protest both nights. Steak, baked potatoes, and red, red wine for the first night's meal would restore our frames and frames of mind.

After we passed under the nature trail footbridge the canal went due west for almost a mile and then veered northwest. By the time we got to the direction change, we had our strokes synced and a good natural feel for the calm, tea-colored water we would be in for three days. We were paddling side by side and Chase spoke first.

"Mom said Alex was up ahead."

"That's what your dad told us," I replied. "I figured he would be too stove up for something like this after his fight with Tucker. He sure doesn't have broken ribs if he can paddle a canoe. My rear end is spittin' washers from the strain and I'm healthy."

Hamp looked around again as if he was not sure I was straining. My left hand was gripping the top of the paddle and I waved with my middle finger.

Alex's round trip to Canal Run would be about twenty miles—a pretty good jaunt for a solo canoeist in questionable condition. Midday, the sun beats down with a purpose and the playful wind claims the flat terrain for its very own. Stiff breezes are more cooperative on the return trip and, as if trying to clear their playground of intruders, nudge the backs of boaters to their starting point.

Our trail to Round Top branched eastward from the canal two miles beyond Bugaboo Island and would be marked by unobtrusive signs with small purple canoes mounted on stakes at critical turnoffs and mileage points. Alex's destination was two miles past the purple trail entrance on the canal, but I wondered if he was actually going there.

"Let's go on up to Canal Run and have lunch with Alex," I suggested. "We'll have plenty of time."

We had been going at a good pace judging by the mile marker count and had only stopped twice for photos. Ty and Byron Stone Slappey had about got the hang of forward motion and were snaking up the waterway within screaming distance behind us so we didn't worry about them. We didn't want to arrive too early to make camp on the platform because there could be as much as a five-hour wait until dark. After enjoying the spectacular 360 degree view of the prairie, there was little to do other than nap or have farting contests. I was no match with Jar since he could fart on command, but I was able to sleep on command and preferred to wait until night after we revered the full moon and its spell. I brought real playing cards just in case.

"I'm game," Jar said.

"Me too," added Chase.

Ty and Byron were too far back to consult but as long as they were out of the water, they would surely go along with it. Byron seemed hot for a crack at any thing the trip had to offer but Ty had turned surly after his dip in a foot of water.

Viewed from the back, there was a slight change in the tilt of Hamp's head and square of his shoulders. The mute message was subtle and concise: *Noble, that is two more miles to add to the trip, which makes four miles round trip, and my upper body will be singing the blues tonight even if we were to stop right now. I'll go along with the majority but my lower body may have to kick your ass.* I splashed him with a handful of water and he signaled me with his finger. I loved that guy.

* * * *

Chase was the first to hear the plane.

Chapter 8

The four previous sightings must have made a marked influence on Chase's hearing. Sound carries well in the swamp but it was a good ten seconds before I heard the deep moan of the engine. We were a half mile past the north end of Bugaboo Island and the vista beyond the left side of the canal was clear, allowing almost full exposure of the northwest side of the island. There was no clearly defined bank on that side of the channel and the waters of the vast bog blended with that of the canal at gaps between occasional cypress trees and knees and patches of scrub-shrub growth. Water was exchanged between the waterscapes in a constant give and take and the wake of our boats caused an exaggerated struggle for the tannic-stained liquid to seek balance. We wedged the front of the canoes in some low-growing bushes at the bank and waited. Ty and Byron managed the maneuver with little difficulty and began bailing water they somehow took on since we started. They used a bottomless milk jug that Aunt Julia insisted they take along.

"I don't see it yet," I said as I stood carefully. My shins braced on the thwart in front of me and helped me balance.

Chase kept his seat and craned his neck. "He flies so low, you won't see him until he gets nearly to the island. Keep your eye on the far end over those tall pines."

Suddenly, there it was, just as Chase had described before. The door was latched open and a bag appeared, beginning its descent. A small parachute deployed almost immediately and interrupted the forward trajectory, allowing the package to fall lazily out of sight into the pines. Immediately after freeing the load, the plane banked toward the Stephen Foster State Park entrance to the northwest and went briefly out of sight. The Cessna reappeared after a few seconds on the far side of the wide loop it made and headed for the route it came in on beyond the island. We sat quietly as the engine sound faded to nothing.

Chase started pushing off the bushes. "Well, let's go check it out."

"Whoa!" Jar cried. His paddle still rested crossways on the cooler. "We're not putting a foot on that island. How do you know they are not gathering up the delivery right now? They'll be armed and constantly alert if this is a drug drop. There could be close to two million dollars worth of drugs in that size bag and those fellas will be real proud of it. We need to notify Bill Becker and let him get direction from the refuge manager. They may want to get some outside help on this."

The bailing stopped. "What's going on, guys?" Ty asked.

Chase held on to a limb to keep from drifting. "Jar, you're the outside help—you've helped them before with lawbreakers. Besides, how are you going to notify them? We made you leave your cell phone at home."

"He's right, Jar," I said. "We need to check it out. The plane flew toward the west entrance to signal the drop, so it will be a while before the pickup is made. Besides, it may not even be drugs."

"You can bet your favorite cap it's something illegal, Stone. What else of value could they be dropping in that size package? Guns? Too small. Stolen jewelry? Too big. Money or gold? That can change hands in easier and safer ways. One thing's for sure—that guy wasn't target practicing."

"Fellas, what's this all about?" Ty repeated. "I thought we were in Folkston, not Memphis. "This sounds like some major shit on the toilet seat. Are we fixin' to sit in it?" He was starting to get pissed.

Jar, Hamp, Chase and I sat a few moments thinking it over. Our recent conversation had to be a major surprise to Ty and Byron. Their annual visits had to be a welcome respite from big city life and the pressures of the used car industry—it was for Hamp and me too, even from a friendly college town. Each time they came I could see them embrace the simpler, primitive life south Georgia had to offer and the role they assumed while visiting was primarily one of passive observing rather than active participating in that life. Ty even avoided the arduous games of horseshoes. Last year they stayed two extra days after the reunion and seemed content to spend their time on the Stone's Throw pavilion drinking sweet tea and watching lazy ducks swim in the pond while the rest of us were on a day or overnight trip getting sunburned, insect bit, and muscle pained. This year they found themselves on one of those strenuous flat-water canoe trips in the harsh wilderness and were witness to what we were claiming to be a drug drop. They had every right to know what was going on.

Chase gave a quick, comprehensive recap starting with the several plane sightings. He mentioned the pictures he took and told how Hamp and I got involved by developing them and transporting them south under the surveillance and threat of interception by Safepoint Security. The account of the break-in and shootings at home in Athens made his explanation of my theory of a major drug operation even more believable. When Chase finished the short narrative, their reaction compasses pointed different ways.

"Well let's go check it out," Byron said. "How do we get there? I've got to piss a boot-full anyway and I can't figure how to do it in this bucket without being lunch for that 'gater over there." There was a six-footer across the canal watching our every move. "There's not enough of me to hang it over the side."

Ty turned around to face him with a scowl. "Well, Mr. Numb-Nuts, I'm surprised you realized we were almost 'gater bait back at the landing. If you ask me, Mother Nature is going to be dangerous enough out here without us going after drug dealers too. I'm ready to go back."

"Fuck you, Ty," Byron said before he spat in the reddish-brown water. "I'm just as out of my element out here as you are but I'll be damned if I spend vacation this year sitting around at Uncle Hank's feeding ducks and swatting flies like we've been doing every year. We need to take separate vacations like we used to. Hell, we have an apartment together, we work together and we go on vacations together. We even married into the same family and divorced the same year. I don't know about you, but I'm getting a life that doesn't involve checking to see if you are around every minute."

That had to have felt better. I had no idea of the tension between them but I tried to think of times when I didn't see them together and it started to make sense. Dad always said that his sister didn't range far enough from the pile of Stones near the swamp to keep static out of the family line and he usually said it when Ty and Byron was involved in something that required county emergency services, hospitals, or lawyers. He was careful to share that again out of the earshot of Aunt Marla when the Chrysler exploded the day before. She had come on a bus separately from her sons for her annual two-week visit to kin in the area. Uncle Graham always stayed in Memphis to tend to the used car business.

I thought the guys simply didn't mesh. Dad was being unfair, considering none of our relatives, including me, saw fit to call 911 during the car fire bedlam and that the simple act entailed presence of mind that Dad claimed was completely lacking in my cousins. I also thought he might be bitter about the poly wheelbarrow melting and he would have to assemble another one when he bought it.

Ty and Byron just sat, steaming.

Chase had a good idea. "We could wait and nail them when they pick up the goods and return to the canal. We can't paddle to the south end of the island with this load anyway."

"Nope, I'm not putting you guys in that kind of danger. We would lack the element of surprise in these sluggish bright canoes. I'm also not going to harass citizens that are technically not in my jurisdiction. I can't go around challenging people on federal land and inspecting their luggage without just cause."

The five of us were staring at Jar and he gave a weak smile when he realized what he said. Sure, there was just cause—two mil in drugs. He undid a compartment in his pack and pulled out his service revolver and a box of ammo. "Can we make it to the near end of Bugaboo without unloading? If so, we'll walk its length to get to the drop point."

* * * *

We had been to Bugaboo Island years ago. It was two and a half miles long and varied from a mile to a mile and a half wide. Its length was split in half by a branch running east and west through the middle of it. On each side of the branch was a small oak grove and near the oaks in the coarse sandy soil were two ancient burial mounds said to have been there well before the Seminoles arrived. There were game trails everywhere and they would normally be easy to travel when fires kept the undergrowth burned off, but there apparently had been several growing seasons since the last fire and the going would be tough.

There was a small open area on the tip of the island and the water was deep enough to pull the three canoes on the bank alongside each other. We welcomed the chance to stretch our legs after the struggle through the shallow, narrow 'gator trails lined with clumps of grass, golden club, and bladderworts. Wildflowers had started to bloom in March, and in April, many orchids and insect-eating pitcher plants had begun their show of color and new growth and claimed their space in the water and on peat deposits. We were definitely off the beaten path, and the depthless water trail and encroaching side vegetation made our half-mile battle to the island take a full hour to win. Our method of travel still beat the old way of traveling in the swamp, which was wading from knee deep to arm pits in the marsh or jumping from one clump of vegetation to another.

Before the jungle hike, we quickly ate a Snickers bar and drank the water melted from our frozen milk jugs that served to cool our food and drinks and doubled as a source of drinking water. We were tired and soaked with sweat from the ordeal getting from the canal to Bugaboo and thought it wise to replace liquids and energy before starting out on foot. We also sprayed liberally with insect repellent for the mosquitoes, chiggers and deer ticks that surely lurked in the damp, dark copse of trees. After Ty considered the heat and distance to the far end he decided to stay with the canoes and gear and rest. I had hoped Byron would offer to stay with him but that wasn't likely after their little spat. He insisted on going even after being warned of the rough going ahead. They had no stake in the unfolding drama and there was no need to subject them to possible danger and difficult travel, but I could understand them not wanting to be together for a while.

If we hadn't lingered those few minutes, and if I hadn't stepped around some trees to pee, I wouldn't have noticed the canoe partially hidden behind scrub brush.

Chapter 9

Bugaboo Island got its name in 1874 during a second trip there by pioneer Josiah Mizell. He had discovered the island on his first trip deep into the swamp, and on the second visit, took some hunting buddies, since the place abounded with game—particularly deer and black bear. Turkeys were plentiful too. The men even built a small earth-floored cabin for shelter on their many subsequent trips there for food. One of the hunters returned to camp early one afternoon and anxiously told a story of hearing a fearsome sound like a bull booing, or bellowing, near where he was hunting. The group's first thought was that it was a 'gator claiming his territory, but mating season didn't start until April and the men were there in the fall. Also, the reptile's bellowed warnings were usually followed by a kind of growling sound and the hunter said he hadn't heard that. He was so earnest in telling his story, and obviously frightened by the experience, that the rest of the hunters went back with him to his deer stand to try to determine what he had heard. After looking around, they found that the eerie sounds were made by two trees rubbing together when the wind blew. Needless to say, the hunters ragged the guy about his "booger" and "booing" and the name Bugaboo resulted from the incident.

I could understand the poor hunter's spookiness. The heavy growth of spectral trees and bushes allowed little light to penetrate the gloominess, and the ghostly silence caused us to want to speak softly, our voices hollow and unnatural. The meandering game trails helped tremendously with our progress through the thick, dark undergrowth to the far end of the island, though we had to bend over much of the time. The resulting lack of clear vision and vulnerable position helped fill me with doubt and uncertainty of what was around the next bend and, in some places, of what was an arm's length away.

We had confirmed that the hidden canoe was one from the rental fleet at the concession area and knew Alex was somewhere ahead of us, but we were unsure of his role, if any, in getting the duffel to the west entrance of the swamp. I checked the six-pack size cooler Chase's mom fixed for him and found two empty cans and the wrappers from two sandwiches and potato chips floating among the remaining ice. If the stash he was after was cocaine, that size container had to weigh close to a hundred pounds and he would need all the energy he could summon, though he would still have to drag it. It would be next to impossible for him to carry that weight the two and a half mile length of the island on trails he could seldom walk erect on. Besides, the trail we were on didn't look traveled by humans so there must have been better access closer to the south end of island where the drop was made. We would have some answers when we caught up with him.

I hoped we were right in assuming the pick up crew wouldn't leave the Stephen Foster State Park until the plane signaled them. Winds and inclement weather, as well as other things unforeseen, could vary the flight time to Bugaboo by several hours, making it impossible to predict an exact arrival time. I decided flexibility was the key to making an operation like that work right and recognizing a weak link like perfect timing kept the chain of events from breaking. Making radio contact to announce estimated arrivals would be risky because transmissions, even in code, could be monitored and questioned, so rather than wait for the delivery in the heat of the swamp, they could wait in air-conditioned comfort until the plane made the loop over them as a signal. The package would be safe on the far end of rugged unpopulated terrain until they got there.

I still couldn't help but worry about that. If they were nearby, it would be hard to sneak up on them brushing and stomping through the spiny thickets.

Thankfully, the going got easier as we approached the halfway point. The thick pines and low growing vegetation gave way to an old oak grove, near which was two large Indian mounds easily noticed by the abrupt change in grade and elevation. The ground in the area was coarse gray-white sand with very little living or rotting vegetation as opposed to the thick organic matter we had just traveled on. I could only guess that winter winds blasted across the island through the leafless oak trees and swept the marl clean. We skirted the graves and paused at what the swampers called a branch that divided the island and we looked for a narrow place to cross without getting too wet. There was no noticeable current in the narrow channel. It was stained the same dark tea color as the open waters by acids from decaying vegetation. The liquid pulsed slowly in one direction, then in the other, as if controlled by sluggish heartbeats at each side of the island. We found a narrow place to cross and a deep footprint on the far side told us that Alex had recently jumped across at the same point. Beyond the stream, a winter fire had burned the heavy growth among the trees, and the small shoots of new growth would not hamper our progress the rest of the way.

I kept a subconscious eye out in case Jar removed a pack of peanuts or M&M's from his shirt of many pockets and programmed myself to be near him with hand out if he did. I didn't live to eat like I sometimes thought Jar did, but I certainly ate to live, and after the jungle trek, tree bark had started to look good. It wouldn't have been nearly as bad if Chase had not shared the trip's tantalizing menu with us the night before, but I was starting to think of the dry bags and coolers full of delicious food and drink that we left over a mile of knuckled vines and roots behind and of what difference another few minutes would have made if we had lightened the cargo by having a couple of sandwiches. Chase thought to take his camera bag and I wondered why one of us didn't have the forethought to pack a bag of food.

Our situation called for action, however, and we needed to move quickly to interrupt any plans of transferring the package to its next destination. I definitely questioned Alex's lone role in that step and, in spite of my hunger and weakness, tried to remain alert to the possibility of other visitors to the target area. Jar's estimate of the street value of that size bag was nearly two million and I doubted that an organization would skimp on manpower to move such a payload without backup or a backup plan. Alex by himself would be skimping if he was part of their plan.

We made good time past the branch, and the small oak grove gave way to pines again. It was not as dark and foreboding as the first half of the journey, but dusky feelings remained with us as we neared the destination. We walked abreast several feet apart and threaded our way through the fire-charred trees. Within a hundred yards, we came upon four deer scattered about feeding on tender shoots that peeked through the blackened floor of the forest. Two newborn fawns were almost invisible with their camouflaged coats. The adults stared at us momentarily and, confident we were no threat, went back to their browsing.

The sun was past the mid-afternoon point and I contemplated our itinerary after we intercepted the package and confronted the ones that would come to pick it up. It would be well after dark if we returned to the east entrance, but if Jar arrested any bad guys, we would have to take them in immediately. I had pretty much given up on the camping trip after the plane was spotted, so we would focus on the task at hand and plan as the puzzle came together. I wondered if it would be appropriate to rest and have a picnic supper with prisoners before taking them in. I was worn out and hungry.

* * * *

After hiking a mile or so past the branch, or wet swale that divided the island, we could see additional sunlight pouring through the pines to the forest floor about three hundred yards ahead. We agreed that was probably the open target area and decided to spread out until we reached that point in case the clearing was missed in the drop. In doing so, we would meet up with Alex sooner and determine what his interest was in Bugaboo's secrets. Hamp took the far left side, Jar and I the center, and Chase and Byron took the right. At three to four hundred feet apart, we covered most of the width of the island at that point. Without the thick undergrowth, visibility was good and we passed quietly through the pines, being careful to keep each other in sight and an eye out for visitors.

We closed in at what we assumed was the drop sight and found it to be only a two hundred foot natural clearing of irregular shape. The ancient remains of log sills outlining the hunting cabin of pioneer Josiah Mizell and his buddies were barely visible in the space, and would soon be gone without a trace, even in human memories and written accounts. Time seemed to control everything and, given enough of it and what it allowed, eliminated all but wispish hints of the past—most of which would never be found. Remains of cultures actually discovered by the learned were often filed away in boxes and drawers, and accounts of the discoveries if read by common folk like me were as dry as the dust that covered them. Artifacts and human remains we were privileged to view in sealed, glass-covered containers in museums could be thousands of miles from their resting place and, to me, lost their significance and authenticity in the transfer.

I liked to read life into what I saw and spent the moments we stood there imagining friends and family around campfires late into the night, sipping home brew and sharing real experiences and tall tales, or perhaps planning a prank on a pal that went to bed too soon. They were genuine participants in life and their wins and losses were not assigned a number as in a video game or on a payroll check; they were rewarded with understanding and increased passion for life that simplicity allowed. Many people now only get to see the lifeless tags on pieces of bone and pottery behind cold glass and reflections of fluorescent lights and the existence and purpose of those things become harder and harder to warrant.

Thunder rumbled in the west and alerted us to continue our journey. There was no duffel in the pines for the past several hundred yards, so we spread out again to cover the last half-mile of the island, being careful to check for a tree that might have interrupted the landing. Each thunderous warning of the fast approaching storm was louder than the previous one, giving little indication that it would play out or pass us by. We would be getting the full force of it within thirty minutes.

We quickly made it to the far end of the island where it yielded to the wetlands, and wading birds registered complaint that we were nearing their rookeries and interrupting their schedule of feeding their young. There was no sign of a bag or parachute. We rejoined on Chase's side near the clearing and faced west, watching the thunderstorm approach. The charcoal gray wall of rain was veined with intermittent lightning all across the horizon. There was even less chance now that it would die out or go around us in the ten minutes or so it would take to get to us.

"We should head for the oaks, I guess," Jar said. "They're not as tall as the pines and maybe won't attract as much lightning. They'll give more shelter too. Sitting in that small clearing among the pines doesn't seem that safe to me."

Chase was looking to the right, toward the north. "Looks like we are going to have more to visit us than the storm." He had telephoto lens attached to his camera and snapped a couple of shots as he looked.

A dark square-stern canoe had become visible and I could make out two figures paddling hard to make the island before the storm. The motor was tilted up, useless in the wet grassy prairie. Judging by the direction they came from, it looked like they had left the Canal Run waterway near the Canal Run Shelter and were making their way among the weeds and around peat blowups straight toward us. I could almost plot their route among the obstacles from our elevated vantage point. It was not straight, but it appeared to be the deepest water and easiest going, and was probably the same route taken for each pickup. They would make the two-mile meandering trip to the lower end of the island where we were in less time than it took us to reach the northern end through 'gator trails only a half-mile from the canal.

We hurried to the oak grove, being careful that our movement wouldn't be spotted by the canoeists. Chase wanted to get pictures of them closer up, so we picked a location in the grove on the west side and tracked their progress toward the landing while behind trees and spotty growth near the water. The trip there completely winded Jar and Byron and they stood bent with hands on knees drawing great gulps of air. Hamp and I were recovering with less fanfare but still had to breath through our mouths. Chase's lips were pursed in photographic concentration.

The storm was introduced by a brief show of wind, and then a short heavy spray of huge drops pounded down like liquid marbles. After a ten-second hesitation the wet drab wall hit with full intensity, drowning out all but the closest claps of thunder. Lightning brightened the iron-gray water world to a sudden intense white and thunder slammed us like giant cupped hands clapping our bodies.

We took off our caps and shirts and let the cold torrent rinse the sticky oils and sweat from our hair and skin. The trees only slowed the rain's descent, and once they were saturated, allowed full flow to us and to the ground. We welcomed the refreshing bath though, and momentarily forgot that the population of Bugaboo had increased by two.

* * * *

The deluge lasted nearly thirty minutes. There was a pause, and then lighter rain came from higher clouds for another quarter hour. The thick leaves of the oaks were able to shed most of the light rain and we lingered under the trees for more rest. Invisible wind and water currents caused random shiny streaks on the dull rain-spattered surface of the swamp and they looked like huge stretch marks on a flattened, once-fat tummy.

As the rain came to an end, Chase caught occasional movement of the newcomers in the distance with his camera lens and he moved about sideways for short distances seeking clear sight through the thick pines.

"Looks like they've started looking for the bag. I can barely make them out, but they appear to be medium size, one maybe taller than the other. They have on long pants and light colored short sleeve shirts and both have dark caps—probably baseball. They started looking around the clearing first and are looking beyond it now. I guess they'll be headed this way soon. I hope I'm wrong, but one of them has something slung over his shoulder and it looks like an assault rifle. It's not a camera bag, I know that."

"What can we do, Jar?" I asked. "If they don't find the drugs or whatever is in the bag, we can't pin that on them and take them in. We'll just spook them and whoever they work for and their whole operation will be changed. We need to stop them for good."

"You're right. If we stopped them now, which I'm not sure we could do anyway if both are armed, I could get them for having weapons in the Refuge, but that won't stop the flow of drugs. They'll just find another route and go unpunished. The drugs are still on the island and will eventually be found by them so I think we should wait. The problem is, we'll be found too if we don't get into thicker cover. It'll be dark before long and they'll surely call off the search for the night."

"Where are they now?" Hamp asked Chase.

"About midway of the island on this side of the clearing. They're ranging farther from the drop point now and are presently headed to the east side. I think one of them just made a cell phone call. He paced back and forth a minute or so and waved one arm frantic-like in the air."

Chase continued to post us on their movements. They swung in ever widening arcs from left to right and back again, drawing nearer with each sweep. The sun made one last appearance between straggling clouds before its descent into the horizon. Chase couldn't tell if they had flashlights to continue their search so Jar suggested we head back through the undergrowth to the canoes to be safe and plan the next step.

We stood and waited while Chase put away his camera. His last report was that the two men were walking to the left with their backs to us, so it was time to move out. They probably couldn't have seen us with the naked eye from that distance, but they might have noticed movement if they faced us.

I looked around for Hamp but didn't see him. I was about to say something to the others when something on the water to the right caught my eye. The dark canoe that was beached near the clearing was headed away from the island with a sole occupant paddling like mad in the dimming light. It was Hamp.

"Oh, shit," I said as I continued to stare.

Jar and Chase must have followed my gaze, and from behind me I heard them say the same thing in unison. Byron stared in amazement and confusion.

Chapter 10

During the hellish struggle through the overgrown trail back to the canoes, I considered how long Hamp might have thought about his plan to steal the bad guys' boat, and I wondered if he thought this caper completely through.

The men had been on the island only a few hours and a big part of that was in a mind-numbing thunderstorm. Jar and I had discussed that they shouldn't be allowed to continue their drug smuggling operation, but the only strategy we came up with was to wait until the drugs were found and nab them with the goods. With dark coming on we had no choice but to fall back to safer territory for the night and resume our watch at first light the next day. One glaring problem to me was that we had them outnumbered but they had us out-armed, and unless we came up with a sure-fire plan to overcome them, our remains could be joining those in the Indian mounds.

At one point, Hamp had asked Chase about the whereabouts of the guys, so he must have planned his move for when they were on the far side of the island. The landing place for their canoe was shielded by tall weeds and shrubs and his departure would have gone unnoticed. In fact, it was possible they wouldn't notice the canoe was even missing until the next day unless they needed something from it, and it was doubtful they brought much for a quick in-out trip. If they did happen to notice it was gone, it would be a simple matter for them to call for help from their cell phone, but the public park where they came from didn't open until seven. It would be late morning before help arrived and that would buy us a lot of time plus add some more villains to the pot.

Maybe Hamp did think it through.

*   *   *   *

We never dried out from the rain and our trip to the top end of the island just soaked us more from sweating and brushing against wet leaves and branches. Luckily, Chase and I had on our Tevas and we didn't have to put up with our feet squishing in shoes like Jar did. He claimed to have at least two blisters and in addition to stumbling from hunger and exhaustion, he limped to compensate for the blisters on his feet. Byron never complained a bit about his sodden tennis shoes.

We tried a different path on the return trip but the going was no easier than our trip in. When we finally made it to the canoes, the five of us headed for the coolers and food. Ty sleepily emerged from the tent he had pitched after we left him and assessed our bedraggled clothes and bodies, probably thankful he didn't go with us. He never asked us how it went and we didn't offer anything. I drank the melted water from a milk jug and two cokes before I started with the food. I could have sworn I heard Jar growl in our scramble in the packs but it might have been my complaining stomach. We had plenty of fixings for sandwiches including mayo and mustard, but packaged ham on bread worked just fine. I took the time to add sliced cheese to my third sandwich for variety and even took the extra time to chew that one. The main course took ten minutes and a double pack of Oreos split five ways took another ten.

It was well after dark by the time we finished eating and Chase broke out his headlamp and two flashlights. We used them sparingly, not knowing whose attention we might draw, and re-secured the packs after dousing with insect repellent again. Chase took out two tent ground covers and spread them in the small open space near the canoes and we sat quietly pondering our situation. I deferred to Jar and Chase to get the ball rolling on a plan because I was too tired to think.

"We need to do several things right away," Jar began. "First, we have got to get off this island to some place safer. There are already two men here and they are bound to have guns. More will likely come tomorrow and we wouldn't stand a chance. "Second, we should hook back up with Hamp as soon as possible. He has probably made it to the canal by now and will be headed back toward us. He'll never see the way in here in the dark, so we could meet him on the canal and go either to the Canal Run overnight shelter or Coffee Bay day use shelter where it will be more comfortable and some of us can get some sleep. Third, one of us needs to go to the east entrance and call Bill Becker with the Wildlife Service and my dispatcher for help. Since Hamp took the canoe, the guys stranded here will have another boat and reinforcements here sometime in the morning and I'm certain they will all be well armed.

"What do y'all think? Is it a plan?"

"Sounds good to me," Chase said. "I'll go for the help—you geezers wouldn't make it."

"In my case, you're right about that," Jar agreed. "What do you say, Noble—ready to get started?"

"It's a pretty good plan, I guess, but there's one problem and you guys won't like my solution to it."

"What's that?" Jar asked.

"As much as I want for us to get back together in a safe place, I'm not leaving this island until I find Alex."

* * * *

I was so tired—too tired to sleep. I lay alone in the two-man tent staring through the mesh roof at stars whose glow would soon be diminished by a full moon and its brightness on sky and land. I needed that light for my journey. I could hear Byron stirring about outside, sleep avoiding him too.

Jar, Chase, and Ty had been gone an hour. They had settled on staying at Coffee Bay Shelter on the canal after they met up with Hamp. At first, they were reluctant to leave us on the island, but they finally admitted that only Chase had the stamina to paddle for help and that Jar did not have it to search the dense vegetation for Alex. We would all assemble at the shelter until Chase returned with help. None of the drug people would be going near there. Byron had insisted on staying with me to help get the loaded canoe out when I found Alex. I could have emptied the canoe and come back for the things another day, but it was obvious he was starting to enjoy our little adventure and wanted to be close to any action. I would be safe enough on the search if I stayed on the north half of the island where Alex was bound to be since we didn't see him in the burned-out section of the pines. Byron agreed to stay and watch the camp and paddle to safety in Alex's canoe to get help if we didn't return by daybreak. Otherwise, after finding Alex and resting, we would make our way to the canal by morning and meet up with Jar, Hamp and Ty at Coffee Bay to wait on the reinforcements.

We had all agreed that Alex should be found and helped if he wanted or needed it and we were ashamed that he was almost forgotten until the last minute. After discussing it, we were convinced that he wasn't in on the drug smuggling since he didn't connect with the two men when they beached near the drop point. I also doubted that he had his own agenda with the drugs, though he might know where they were. After his scrap with his brother the day before and the arduous trip alone to Bugaboo in his condition, he was probably near exhaustion.

As I lay there, my thoughts turned to the swamp and the role it had played in people's lives. Over the years the Okefenokee has been a source of many things that brought comfort and life to some, agony and death to others. Long ago, a railroad was built deep into the swamp from the west edge and the inhabitants of Billy's Island near there grew from Dan Lee's family of sixteen to more than six hundred. In 1909, logging operations with the growing work force began supplying timber throughout the Southeast and beyond for homes, factories, bridges, and endless other uses. The operations ceased in 1927 but not before over four million board feet of timber were removed that could otherwise have provided shelter and harbored food for wildlife, among other roles in the ecosystem.

Wild game abounded then and provided settlers in and around the swamp with a seemingly endless supply of meat, but trapping of the game for fur was taking a heavy, cruel toll on the animal population for the vanity of a few thoughtless outsiders. Over time, hundreds of trappers and thousands of neglected traps caused slow, suffering deaths to helpless animals. I blamed the final owners of the furs more than I did the trappers because they kept the fashion going that encouraged the greed and slaughter. We have only recently come to our senses and begun to realize that the real beauty of fur is on the original owner.

Now the swamp was being used as a conduit for illegal drugs. I still had to blame the final owner and user though they suffer the most. The health, lives, and fortunes of so many were lost because of their dependence and the lack of strength and help to end the dependence. Innocent victims suffered the long agonies too, and if the flow of drugs can't be stopped, maybe some day the market will.

So very tired…

* * * *

I awoke to the screams of thousands of frogs. In fact, I fell asleep to them when my thoughts succumbed to my body's call for rest, but they seemed louder now without those thoughts. The sound was like a pulsing blend of high pitches that punctuated a horror scene in an old Hitchcock movie. I sat up far enough to prop on my elbows and confirmed that my back, shoulders and arms had a scream of their own from yesterday's exertion. Byron was next to me in deep sleep. I checked my watch with a brief flick of a flashlight and it was after midnight, the South Moon still on its rise in the cloudless sky. Old time swampers gave a rising moon that name and claimed that during that period was the best hunting. At least it's light would help in my hunt for Alex.

I washed two Little Debbie cakes and three aspirin down with a canned iced tea drink and selected quick-drying shorts and a tee shirt from my pack. I had stripped off my wet clothes and put on clean boxer shorts a few hours earlier while the others changed and prepared to leave for the canal. Jar had added a sleeping bag and a change of clothes for Hamp to their already heavy load before leaving.

I chose to wear my sandals again for the ventilation and fast drying, and found the dry Suwannee Canal baseball cap I had packed that Chase had given me last Christmas. I had given him a Georgia Dawg cap and I noticed he was wearing it when they left. After applying insect repellent and stuffing two Sigg liter-size bottles of drinking water and some energy bars in a small pack, I slipped quietly away allowing Byron to continue his much-needed sleep.

* * * *

After the drug drop the day before, we had landed on Bugaboo Island at the top end on the left, or east side, and took trails on that side through the stubborn thicket that prevailed on the first half of the journey. On the way back that evening, we tried the west side and it was the same rough going. I chose a route close to center for the nighttime trip and used the moon, which was not yet at its high point, to help me with direction. I would split the difference between the middle trail and the previously traveled trails for other passes in my search if they were required. The game trails mostly crossed the land lengthwise but were by no means direct routes and I would have to zigzag with them. When I found Alex he would surely be on a trail because the rest of that end of the island was a tangled mass of vines and sharp briars and fronds.

The area I had to cover was only about two square miles, but if I had to cover it all, it would be a slow painful process. The shadows from the bright moon on the wild growth caused me to misjudge steps, dodges, and ducks, and my bare legs, arms and face were scratched without mercy. After thirty minutes of the grueling search, I had to rest.

I stopped in a space where I could stand upright and drank some water. I wondered how much longer I could go. The measure of reaching my destination would be made by when, in time, I found my cousin. Distance had little significance on the meandering course other than its physical toll on me. I was probably only four hundred yards from camp as the crow flies, and I shuttered to think of the distance I would travel over the knitted hank of exposed roots for the one-mile crow flight to the branch. I hoped it wouldn't take all night.

After the rest break, I took three steps and tripped and fell to the ground over Alex's body.

Chapter 11

Alex looked like shit. After I recovered from the fall and realized what caused it, I turned him over on his back and he grunted but remained motionless. The moonlight making it through the shadowed veil of growth around us revealed that one side of his face had deep creases from lying on dead vegetation on the uneven ground, and both sides were dirty and scratched. His long dark hair was damp and matted and had debris on the side that had touched the ground. Dark spots of old blood spotted his once-white tee shirt at several rips and his long khaki pants had bad tears on both knees. Some of the scratches on his arms looked bad enough to bleed but it was apparently washed off when it rained earlier. His blackened left eye from his fight with Tucker was in shadows, but it appeared that the swelling had gone down. The split lip still had swelling and a fresh drop of blood on it shined in the moonlight. His pale skin in that light made him look like a cadaver.

"Alex, can you talk?"

I started to shake him but thought better of it. He looked like one big hurt.

"Alex, try to raise up a little."

I took a bottle of water from the pack and unscrewed the cap. With my left hand under the back of his head, I slowly raised it, slipping my left knee under my hand for support. I touched the bottle to his lips and poured out a little water. When he opened wider, I tilted the bottle more and he started drinking. The water was still ice cold and when some spilled down his chin onto his chest, he drew in a deep breath and choked a little, then poised for more.

"Slow down, Alex, or it will make you sick." I gave him a few heavy pulls on the bottle, then withheld it so the liquid could warm inside him and not cause stomach cramps. The process was repeated until the liter of water was gone.

"Alex, can you sit up?" My left leg had gone to sleep and I needed to get into the pack for more insect repellent. During the earlier trips through the shrub thickets I picked up at least a dozen chigger bites under my arms, at my waistline and parts immediately south of that, even though I had used repellent. My sweat and the rain must have washed it away. It was too late for those bites but I could guard against more with another good spraying. I also thought I had some deer ticks but it was hard to tell with all the scratches and muscle soreness and tiredness competing for attention. I would have to check for them in the daylight. I hated those things.

My immediate problem was that I had missed the back of my neck completely when I started out earlier and the mosquitoes were having a feast. I was slapping myself silly in futile attempts to keep them from biting. In the moonlight I could see a dark cloud of them over Alex in a holding pattern waiting for a chance to land and drink.

"I think so," he rasped. He groaned involuntarily with the challenge and held his right hand to his left side for support against pain of the struggle.

I found the spray bottle and quickly put repellent on my hands to rub on my ears, face, and the back of my neck and followed with a light misting everywhere else, including up the legs of my shorts. I was such a close companion to pain at that point I barely recoiled from the smart. "Want some of this?" I asked. "It'll sting like hell in the scratches but it'll keep the mosquitoes away." I pumped some on his outstretched hand and he clumsily dabbed it on the places on his face that didn't hurt to touch. While he did that, I sprayed a mist on his arms and tee shirt as he sucked in air from the burn of the chemicals.

"Any more water?" Alex managed. He seemed a little self-conscious over his pitiful condition but his body out-ranked his mind and needed relief from the thirst.

His discomfort also seemed to bring down his defenses. "I have really fucked up," he confided after starting on the second bottle of water.

"Alex, we don't have to get into that right now. We're both tired and hurting and we need rest. Let's talk tomorrow." I pulled back the wrapper of an energy bar and handed it to him.

"Noble, this is major," he said before taking a bite. "There are drugs on Bugaboo and two people with guns are here to get them. We've got to stop all this."

"Do you know where the drugs are?"

"I didn't know what else to do by myself to keep them from taking them, so I buried them in the sand midway of the island near the Indian mounds. I camouflaged the ground well with leaves and straw and rolled a piece of hollow rotten log over the area. I don't think they will find them tonight but they may still be looking for them right now. They'll come this way when they don't find the bag on that end. Just before dark they called for help and it should be here in the morning. Then we're really screwed as far as trying to stop them. We'll be in danger too if we don't get off the island."

"I doubt they'll look long in this tangled mass at night. With help coming when it gets light, they've probably called off the search and are getting some sleep. As soon as you're up to it, we'll head back to my camp and do the same. Do you think they saw you?"

"I don't think so. I was really close to them at the time they phoned for help, but I was able to hide in some undergrowth at the edge of the water. The one on the phone said to bring fresh batteries for a signal locator, so there must be a transmitting device in the bag."

Alex finished the energy bar and handed me the water bottle after taking a long swig. He started to lie down.

"Not here, Alex. Let's get back to camp. We can make a faster retreat off the island in the morning. Chase went for help and we're to meet the others on the canal at daybreak. Hamp got these guys' canoe so they're not going anywhere 'til their help comes. If we don't get in the tent, the mosquitoes, ticks and chiggers are going to eat us alive."

"I don't think I can, Noble. I've had it—just leave me here and I'll come in the morning."

"I'm not leaving you here, Alex. You can do it if you just concentrate on one step at a time. You're stiff now—once you get going it will be easier."

I helped him to his feet and as soon as he got his balance, I ducked into the undergrowth and slowly started back, looking over my shoulder to make sure he was following.

"One step at a time, Alex—think about it that way."

* * * *

Sleepless again, I lay in the tent watching the full moon, now at its apex, and lined it up with a seam of the mesh roof and followed its progress across the peaceful blue sky. It traveled surprisingly fast when tracked like that and I guessed its shadows would be gone before the morning shadows took their place. I was glad Ty had not installed the waterproof fly when he pitched the tent because it allowed whispers of breezes that made the damp night air more bearable. Byron never stirred when Alex and I squeezed in beside him when we returned. It had taken us forty-five minutes to get back to camp. Alex peeled off his dirty wet clothes first thing and slipped into a pair of gray sweat shorts I dug from my pack. As soon as his head hit the floor of the tent, he was sound asleep.

As I lay in the small space near him listening to his long, deep breaths, I was naturally aware of his physical reality, but I began to feel a deeper presence that I never had known before. I allowed myself to think of Alex as something more—something beyond a physical being that I knew must be there, but it was locked away for some reason, the plain package unopened, the status protected.

I seldom threw things away that quit working without first seeking out and removing the recessed screws that held them together and finding out what made them tick. My most recent project was a departed cordless phone that I was sure I could bring back to life like I do old tile grout or scratched and dented chair rail. As soon as the screws were out and as I was separating the two pieces, I accidentally ripped a red wire from an unseen connection and parts started to rattle. If I was defusing a bomb I would have been blown to bits. The next screw I took out allowed other parts, whose location I didn't think to memorize, to go everywhere. Then it went into the wastebasket. I was certain it was a ploy by the manufacturer to make its product user-unfixable.

I was thinking I would try the same thing with Alex—get him to open up and see what made him tick—without causing more damage of course. Surely he wasn't as fragile and throwaway as a cordless phone. As far as Chase knew, he had no friends, male or female, to meet and hang out with and his time was spent either working four days a week at Suwannee Canal or part time with an outfitter at St. Mary's and at home caring for his dad. Those things should be a smaller part of his life because at twenty-three he certainly had potential and need for more besides work and living with his dad. There was definitely a life out there without the emotional baggage I knew he was carrying. One day we would discuss it over a couple of six-packs.

My reverie gave way to fitful sleep.

* * * *

It was still dark when noises outside the tent woke me. The moon had a dimmer glow through its longer path in the earth's atmosphere as it descended to the western horizon. It would provide another hour or so of light but it would be several hours before morning light started its shift in the east. I hadn't slept long or well. Painfully, I rolled over and brushed against Alex, feeling heat much greater than the hot night air. He was burning with fever and I could feel it even with my hand inches away from his pale skin. He whimpered and shook his head from side to side several times before settling down again. We were alone in the tent and I lay there a while hesitant to summon the abused muscles that took me to and fro the last twenty hours and wondering which side of my pack I returned the aspirin to earlier. I needed to get some in both of us quick and cool Alex off with something wet. I finally struggled out of the tent with a few grunts that I couldn't hold back and found Byron standing at the canoes, looking north into the blackness toward the canal and mumbling softly to himself. Beyond him, I heard a bump like a paddle hitting the rail of a canoe, then another bump and a muffled curse—it was Jar's voice. I joined Byron and we followed his progress through the shallow trails by the racket, which was amplified by the swamp and the night. The sounds he was making probably carried a mile. The frogs briefly quieted their commotion to hear and feel the intruding vibrations and assess the danger. At one point, the canoe rubbed along a dry root or limb for its entire length and it sounded like nails across a blackboard.

"It's me," Jar said when he got within fifty feet of the bank.

Byron and I helped him pull ashore while he held the flashlight low. The canoe was apparently emptied of gear at the shelter where they were to camp and he didn't seem as wasted as he did the first trip to the island. I went to the cooler and pulled out a canned drink for Jar and a partially frozen jug of water to cool Alex with.

"Alex is bad sick," I said. "He's delirious with fever."

I kneeled at my canoe to look for the aspirin and a cloth to wet and put on Alex.

Jar shook his head and said, "Oh, no. What else can happen?"
"What do you mean?"
"I haven't found Hamp yet."

Chapter 12

"What?" was all I could say. I turned to look at him, still holding a flap to my pack. Just when I thought nothing else would fit in our pocket, I suddenly realized our happy little canoe party was scattered all over the swamp.

Jar's voice was tense and reedy. "When we got to the canal Hamp was not in sight, so I told Chase to drop Ty and the gear off at Coffee Bay and proceed to the recreation area to phone for help. I waited and rested for ten or fifteen minutes and then paddled to the likely place he would come onto the canal but I still didn't see him. I came back, thinking he had bypassed the way into here and that he was probably already at the shelter and I headed there, but no Hamp. I'm wondering now if he kept going past the shelter and went back to the east entrance to call for help."

"I doubt it, Jar. Hamp's more do-it-yourself. If anything, he'll head toward the west entrance at least to Canal Run shelter and hang around to monitor the arrival of the bad guys' reinforcements and to see if he can hinder them."

"Damn, Noble, hindering them is not going to do any good other than risking his life. The perps have to be caught with the goods to make anything stick. Right now, what we have are two men stranded on an island because their canoe has been stolen which makes Hamp the bad guy. Unless they are sitting on the duffel bag full of dope, which happens to be lost right now, when they arrive, the Refuge law guys won't have a thing on them other than possession of firearms in the swamp."

"The bag's been found, Jar." I hated to tell him that because of where it was.

"Huh?"

"Alex found it not long after it landed," I said. "He buried it, trying to keep the pick-up from succeeding. He didn't know we were on the island and did what he thought was right by himself."

"Buried? Shit. Now we sure can't pin the drugs on them. This is getting worse all the time. The two men stranded here are probably from Safepoint Security and will get their hands slapped for the gun charge. They'll have some smoky story to blow up Randy Taylor's lawmen's asses and Hamp could get far more than a hand slapping for stealing their boat and motor. Dad-*gummit.*"

Jar toned down his profanity when he got frustrated. I always assumed it was to keep the harsh words from clouding his thinking and derailing progress toward a solution. Dad-gummit, criminy and blinking were not as invasive as a choice spontaneous cuss word. I always opted for the latter because it let off steam that would otherwise be clouding my own thinking.

I had to get back to Alex. I found the aspirin and grabbed a tee shirt and the jug of ice-cold water and waddled into the tent. He rose and braced with his elbows and took four tablets down with choked swallows. I wet the shirt and slowly laid it onto his white bony chest allowing it to drape down on the bruise on his side. I hoped the fever was just from heat exhaustion and not the result of a cracked rib puncturing a lung. He sucked in air deep and slow from the ice-cold shirt but he didn't resist. As the shirt warmed I added more water until just the fist-sized chunk of ice rattled in the plastic jug. After a while, Alex didn't look as fitful and I could tell his fever was abating.

"The drugs have a signal device packed with them," I said as I sat with Jar and Byron on the ground cloth. "Alex overheard that the rescue party is supposed to bring batteries for a locator so the package can be found. We'll still catch them with the goods if our timing is right."

"Not if Hamp disables the help that's coming," Jar countered. "All he'll accomplish attempting that is to get his own self shot. I can't imagine how he could do it anyway without a gun."

Jar's continued negativity was starting to grate a little but I figured it went with the sheriff's job. So much that he encountered was subject to his criticism and open to his interpretation. I still felt like I should quiet my guilt feelings and take up for Hamp since I frequently accused him of not putting enough thought into some things.

"Hamp's pretty resourceful. In fact, if he can swing it, more help will have to be called for meaning more bad guys to bust. There must be a lot of people involved in an operation this size and the more we can catch red-handed the better. Some will get away regardless, either by not getting ratted on or by running and hiding."

"There's some truth to that, and there's always plea bargaining that can help bring down the ones we don't get. On the other hand, if we spook them too much now they'll abort the project to save all their hides and we will be left with nothing. I'd rather let them find the drugs right away and get the ones we can."

A water bird nearby fussed noisily at our continued chatter and the whoosh of wings flapping told us she sought a more peaceful place to sleep. A slight warm breeze stirred as if coming from the flight but the still swelter soon returned.

"Nobody's going to spook easily with two million in drugs at stake," I said.

Byron spoke for the first time since Jar arrived. "I could sneak in and dig up the bag and put it where the two stranded guys could find it in the morning. That way the wildlife people could nab them with the stuff and get the names of the others—you know, beat it out of them."

I smiled at Byron's simple solution and his eagerness to help. He was definitely a different side of the coin from his brother. Maybe a different coin altogether. Ty was two years older than he was and maybe a brighter nail in the keg so he always called the shots, even in their youth. At thirty, Byron still deferred to big brother who was a hotshot used car salesman and paper work manipulator like his dad and Byron was left with the thankless jobs of gofer, battery charger and car washer. Sometimes he repossessed cars and trucks from easy term defaulters if the vehicle was not gutted and burned or impounded due to the debtor's commission of a crime. The brothers both had a couple of years of college but I would hesitate to loan either one of them power tools. Byron seemed game and keen to learn though and didn't fall as low as the omega male category nor did Ty reach anywhere near the alpha status.

"What do you think, Jar?" I asked. "He's got a point. There's enough moonlight left to get to the buried bag and dig it up."

"What about Hamp?"

"I'll try to find him—I won't be able to rest until I do. Byron can go and dig up the drugs."

"He's going with you. It'll be easier getting to the canal with two people working it and you may need help later. You're too tired to do it alone. I have the gun and I can find the burial site easier than he can. Do you know exactly where Alex buried the stuff?"

I repeated what Alex told me while I threw food, drinks and a first aid kit into my day pack. For good measure, I added my old but barely used Craftsman hunting knife. A big coil of Chase's rope still in Jar's canoe completed our survival gear.

"Where can we get back together, Jar? When we leave you and Alex we'll be split up five ways. We can't just keep hunting one another."

"Come back here. We should be safe enough on this end of the island. By the time I make my trips through the brush I'll be too wasted to paddle out of here with Alex right away. When Chase comes with the help he'll see we're not at Coffee Bay and know this would be the next logical place. That will get five of us back together and Ty will be OK at the shelter. We'll leave together when the refuge people take over."

The human mind thinks, and having thunk, moves on. I thought we had a good plan. You grab it, take out the screws and take it apart until there's nothing left but the answer. I hoped we didn't leave anything out.

* * * *

"Let's do it then!" Byron had exclaimed. He was ready for hair-raising adventure and high-speed drama. I was ready for a long shower, slow back rub and passive twitterpating with Bonnie Gill. Food not encased in bread would be good too.

After checking on Alex, Jar disappeared into the thicket. Byron and I wrestled the canoe around and urged it through the shallow water and deep muck. I took the front this time for better visibility and guided us through the twisting trail. Without the heavy gear we made it to the canal in no time and hung a left toward Canal Run Shelter. The orange moon encased in its aureole still hung low in the night. When it was gone, the darkness would slow our progress even on the wide canal and we didn't want to miss Hamp in case he tied off to the side to sleep.

After nearly two miles, I motioned for Byron to stop. We would be at the shelter soon and I wasn't sure what to expect there. I cautioned him to be as quiet as possible and not bump his paddle against the side of the canoe. He nodded eagerly and we resumed paddling at a slower, more careful pace.

The silhouette of the shelter loomed first and as we got closer, the bank and dock started to take shape. Like most of the shelters there was a narrow wooden platform at the water to dock boats and steep steps from that led to the camping or day use areas. The eighteen-inch risers discouraged alligators from visiting the elevated sites and sunning on the dry decks and land. Human visitors felt a little less intimidated with this arrangement.

We got within a hundred yards and the dark shadows allowed me to recognize the square-stern canoe with the tilted motor. We had caught up with Mr. Slyboots and I was going to give him hell for making us worry while he was peacefully sleeping.

We got closer and I blinked for clarity. No, there were two of those canoes.

Chapter 13

▼

We had stopped paddling and I turned to Byron. He pointed toward the dark shapes and held up two fingers. I nodded in agreement. My sense of foreboding deepened as we eased forward with focused caution. Was one of the dark canoes the one that Hamp stole? If so, the other canoe told me that he was either prisoner of the drug dealers or he had come to harm by them, or both. Our fatigue from the hours since we left the east canal entrance could easily cause carelessness and we could meet the same fate. *Proceed with care.*

Thoughts ran wildly through my mind. What if both of the rigs had brought a rescue team for the ones stranded on Bugaboo? Or, what if one of them had been empty to retrieve the drugs and castaways? It was even possible the canoe theft by Hamp had not yet been discovered and called in. I doubted that one person brought both canoes that far in the middle of the night, so we were up against two, or possibly four, well-armed men. If both boats brought newcomers, we still had to find Hamp, but first we had to be sure he wasn't at the shelter. The only choice was to sneak ahead for a better view. The bank and platform were elevated above the canal and we wouldn't be able to see the occupants unless they were standing near the edge. The moon would soon be gone and then we wouldn't even be able to see that. I was hoping at that time of night they were all asleep. We eased closer, alert for a clue to help us know what we were up against.

* * * *

We were only fifty feet away from the moored canoes when I noticed a paddle laid across the gunwales of the nearest one. That was my sign, deliberate or by accident, that Hamp was there on the platform.

The paddle's perch was a constant complaint of mine with him when we started white-water canoeing in our late teens. My argument was that it could easily slip into the water and be lost to the currents, leaving us crippled if not stranded. It took little more effort to park the thing in the bottom of the boat under the thwarts and I told Hamp that many times.

It was not until after the first time we ran Section Three of the Chattooga River that Hamp started heeding my advice. We had pulled onto a sand bar near the Eye of the Needle rapids to eat lunch and watch capsized canoeists and their gear float downstream. There was a lull in the show but I noticed a lone paddle giving a final wave with its handle before disappearing in the froth below us. There were no distressed paddlers in view upstream that might have lost it, so I suddenly experienced the familiar spasm in my colon. The paddle was Hamp's.

I was able to help a little the rest of the trip by pushing off rocks with a sturdy stick I had found, but Hamp rightfully did most of the work with my paddle. He got us to within a hundred yards of the take-out point before he broke the wooden handle of my Sawyer and we did the last part, including Bull Sluice Falls, outside the canoe trying to propel it and ourselves to shore before we joined the paddles in South Carolina. The banks were lined with onlookers cheering, or maybe ragging, us on. *Assholes.*

* * * *

The placement of the paddle on the canoe was a weak signal but it was the only clue I had to go on at the time. We had to check out the campsite. I eased forward without a sound, Byron following my lead without question. The croaks, chirps and murmurs of night creatures would help mask small noises but a thump or scrape against the dock would be disastrous.

The canoe nearest the steps on the far side was secured fore and aft. The one with the telltale paddle had its bow painter tied to the aft rope of the first boat and it lolled in the canal perpendicular to the bank. I tried not to think of a possible struggle involving Hamp that had resulted in the other line not being secured. When we were parallel to the dock, I stowed my paddle and crept onto the weathered boards to look for something to tie up to while Byron held the craft in place.

I was still in the shadows of the main structure above feeling for a suitable mooring when I heard the distinct sound of a loud fart followed by the splash of liquid on the planks near Byron. Surely he was not pissing and farting at a time like this.

"Son of a bitch!" I heard him yell.

"De fuck?" added a strange voice that sounded confused.

A blinding beam of light flooded over Byron after the brief exchange and it revealed his look of horror with saucer eyes and disgust with a wrinkled nose. I remained frozen to the black shadows, wondering what to do next.

The looming figure must have realized his peter was still out and he hurriedly tucked it in with his free hand. It had stood out in the peripheral light of the beam like an uncooked breakfast sausage.

Without missing a beat, Byron said, "Hell, man, you peed on me! Thank God you're here though. I'm lost as hell and I need to use the shitter something terrible. I got the runs you wouldn't believe. Let me tie up and I'll be right up. Shine the light so I can see the steps. Jeez, I'm glad to see you."

He stomped up the tall steps with exaggerated theatrics. Through the crack in the platform floor, I was aware of another light turning on accompanied by mumbled curses, probably in Spanish.

Byron continued his tirade to the top level and I could imagine the looks of shocked disbelief on the strangers' faces. I was in the same state from his boldness and I couldn't think straight. Finally, a high-pitched voice said, "Chut de fucking up!" It was either the second man or the urinater in a greater state of agitation. I couldn't tell if they had guns out yet.

"Hey, don't get your drawers in a wad, man...and you don't need to point no guns at me. Who's this guy with his hands tied? Is he a criminal?" Byron was giving me information I needed to come up with a plan.

One of the men gave a chilling cackle. "We de crinimals, man, an we gon feed ju bote to de wahder leezards. We choot ju in daybrite an see allegates eat ju penis." Both of them giggled.

The situation didn't have the withering effect on me that I thought it would have. Byron had blustered his way up to the camping deck and was actually carrying on a conversation of sorts with them. Their silliness and lack of control in the situation made me think they were high on something. To stay on top of things, they should have been tying Byron up and keeping him quiet. They still had guns though, and that fact coupled with their poor judgment was a potential deadly combination for him. We needed to be careful. We needed to capitalize on their overconfidence and sense of well-being.

There were some shuffling noises and steps taken. "Shit, man, are you OK? Let me help you stand. What can we do?" Byron had directed the questions to Hamp in a lowered and timorous voice but still spoke so the two men could hear the feigned fear in his voice. Both of them laughed evilly.

"Dere's nutting ju can do, fool. We goin choot ju bote een a leedle wile." They laughed some more.

"I've got a noble plan," I heard Hamp say.

"Chut back up, ju, and seet back down! De noble plin is to die screamin!" More laughter.

"No way noble," the other man theorized, shaking his head.

I became aware of a figure right above me sitting with a thump. When I leaned out and looked up, I recognized the square of Hamp's shoulders. His hands were tied behind him and were within easy reach.

I crawled across the rough boards to where Byron hastily tied the stern to a four by four post and slowly pulled the front end back to the dock. The bow had drifted out toward the middle of the canal and part of it was in the weak wash of light from the flashlights. Easy does it. With my left hand I grabbed the gunwale and pulled the canoe back parallel to the dock. I never had a chance to tie my end off so I made a big loose knot at the right place and laid the painter over the end of the dock boards next to the bank, hoping its draped weight would hold in the still water. We might have to make a quick exit and would need to hop in fast.

Without removing the pack where it lay in the bottom of the boat, I reached down and unlatched one side of the flap and immediately found the hunting knife. The conversation was still going on topside but I barely heard it in my concentration to be quiet. I was also thinking about Hamp saying something about a noble plan. My right knee popped as I stood up and I hesitated a second to make sure it wasn't heard before stepping over to him. I walked slowly as if that would keep the boards from creaking but it didn't. There were a couple of squeaks but they mingled harmlessly with the night sounds and voices above.

Hamp was shirtless and the bonds that I easily cut through appeared to be strips of the shirt he had been wearing. He kept his hands behind him as if he was still tied and I squeezed one of his fists to reassure him before crouching down again.

I had to figure out what Hamp's noble plan might be. *Noble plan...noble plan.*

Hell, it wasn't Hamp's noble plan, it was Noble's Plan!

Look, next time, one of us will distract the bad guy while the other overcomes him. That will be the plan.

Of course. It was the generic plan I had jokingly come up with just two days before to handle the situations we sometimes found ourselves in.

Something distracting. It would have to be striking because the urinater didn't get overly excited when Byron cried out after being splashed upon. I actually thought the guy might have been a little embarrassed when he turned the flashlight on and realized he was still exposed and seen by Byron. If they were the deadhead druggers they sounded like, the more flamboyant the distraction the better to reach those dulled receptors in their nervous systems. Something with fire.

I checked in the first boat for a spare fuel tank and found a square plastic one with a spout and handle. It felt full. Stepping to our rental canoe, I grabbed the book of matches from my pack before freeing the end of it to drift out again. So much for a quick exit—there was only room for two canoes parallel to the dock. I pulled in the middle rig that Hamp had taken so I could get to its extra gas. Hamp hadn't moved from his place near the edge of the platform. I felt around on the deck under him for the cloth strips I had cut from his wrists. I first tied some to the spout of both containers and starting pouring both gallons of fuel in the bottom of the boat at the same time. Careful not to get gas on me or the outside of the cans where I would be gripping them, I emptied them together to save time before the gas smell was detected on the top level.

The next steps would be tricky. I had to push the doused canoe away from the dock so the flames from the explosion of gas and fumes would not engulf me. Then, the matches had to be lit and the gas-soaked rags on the containers ignited. Only one of the two flaming containers would have to land in the spilled fuel in the canoe to do the job, but I felt better having a backup. I was shaking so, I was afraid I would drop the only pack of matches I brought. I needed to shift from my desperate bearing to survival mode without grinding gears.

I untied the end of the canoe and took a death-grip on the book of matches with my left hand. My right hand gave the floating pyre a shove and quickly lit the empty container torches with matches already between my fingertips. I picked them up safely by the grip, one in each hand, and lobbed the first one. It fell short, still burning as it floated in the black water. I already had the second one in my right hand ready to throw. I compensated for the shortfall of the first effort plus allowed for the increased distance the canoe traveled in those few seconds and sent the flame toward the retreating shadow.

WHOOMP!

Now that was a distraction. A giant round ball of fire reached upward and outward and would have reached me and the dock had first torch connected. The conflagration reached across the canal and scorched the leaves on the trees that overhung it. Fiery sparks from them rained down into the reflecting water as the orange ball darkened into a black cloud of smoke and continued rising into the now moon-less night.

The remaining fuel and parts of the canoe above the water line continued to burn and lit up the canal and shelter like flickering gold daylight. The free-floating hull came to rest in the calm water and hung buoy-like. Thankfully, it made no threat of starting an unwanted burn in the swamp. It would soon burn itself out.

After my own reaction to the diversion, I became aware of the activity above me. I had heard a loud yell and a gunshot. A body suddenly fell the six feet onto the edge of the dock near me and rolled into the fire-illuminated water. Two broken rails swung down but remained attached to posts by the nails at their ends. I grabbed the inert form by the back collar and started hauling him up when another gunshot rang out. The man in my grasp was not Hamp or Byron so I dropped him to the planks and scrambled for the steps. When I reached the top I found the remaining three at the back end of the shelter. Byron was straddled over a still, unfamiliar figure, pounding him with one fist and then the other. Hamp lay nearby.

"You goddamned son-of-a-bitch!" Byron cried. "You shot my friend!"

Survival. You can run, hide or put up a fight. Then you emerge and recover and procreate. Survival of the Species.

Chapter 14

Unlike his brother, who was wimpy thin and almost devoid of body hair, Byron was fit and trim and tanned—probably from his manual duties around the car lot. He had long hairy arms and brawny hands but walked upright, contrary to Dad's portrayal. Not long after putting his razor down, he would have a five o'clock shadow and by the end of the day, I was sure his thick black whiskers could shine rusty metal. Deep blue civilized eyes softened his look, though, as did the not-so-prominent brow. Frequently combed black hair and short sideburns confirmed his advanced state.

"By! Don't kill him!" I yelled. I pulled him from the prone body to a standing position but his arms were still thrashing. I twisted him around to face me, and each arm, in turn, stopped swinging.

"We've got to check Hamp, By," I said as I shook him. "Get the pack out of the canoe." I spoke slowly and distinctly like I would to a foreign visitor.

His eyes refocused the short distance between us and after a moment of understanding, he nodded, glanced at Hamp, and scrambled for the steps.

I snatched the still-burning flashlight and shined it on Hamp. He lay on his back, upper arms out to the side with the left forearm angled up and the right pointed down, like half of a swastika. His knees were bent slightly and laying to the left side and his head faced the same way. I had seen the position more than once in movies where the pose was preserved by tracing it with tape or chalk at crime scenes.

Blood had formed a small thick puddle and started making its way through a crack between floorboards. It oozed from a dark hole in the meaty part of his upper arm near the shoulder. I carefully raised him and saw the exit wound underneath with an even greater flow coming from it. I kneaded my own shoulder and judged that the path of the bullet probably missed his bone but it had to go through plenty of muscle mass considering the paddle-induced soreness of mine.

Byron had appeared with the pack and already had the light that was in it out and turned on. He pulled out the bottled water and first aid kit and opened it before speaking. "Is it bad?" He looked anxiously at Hamp.

"I'd say he's damned lucky. This flesh wound is all I could find, but there were two shots, right?" My little distraction even had me distracted.

"Right. The first one went wild. He could have hit the floor pretty hard, though. I was busy slamming Pancho number one over the side—I sure hope I didn't kill him." He couldn't take his eyes off Hamp.

While I cleaned the wound with water and gauze pads, I said, "You didn't. Might pay to check him and get his gun, though. Find Pancho Two's while you are at it and look for the other flashlight—we might need it."

"The light is floating in the canal, still on. I'll get it." He grabbed Two's revolver on the way and disappeared once more down the steps.

I had the bullet holes cleaned and put antiseptic on and around them but I needed to stop the bleeding. I couldn't wrap the gauze too tightly that high up around the arm because it would cut off circulation under the arm. Instead, I made several laps around his chest with the dressing, pulling tight around the outside of the bad arm on thick gauze pads and cradled his lower arm in the sling from my kit to immobilize it.

The entry and exit wounds were three inches apart and that space on the wide pads, and more besides, was saturated with blood. I was not sure it would do any good, but I rolled Hamp onto his left side with his hurt shoulder elevated and his head on the pack. He stirred a little from the movement and opened his eyes.

Byron rejoined us, carrying a bundle under his arm and the missing flashlight. "I couldn't find the gun," he said. "It must be in the canal. We need to get Pancho One up here pretty quick—I shined the light around the water and yellow eyes are glowing everywhere."

"What's that?" I asked, nodding to the khaki bundle.

"One's clothes. We can't take these birds with us, so I figured they'd more likely stay on the platform if their "water lizard" food were exposed and flapping around. Being like that in the water 'peared to rank high on their "terrible fate" list. Also, nobody that happened by would want to help them, them being naked and all."

Made sense to me. I glanced down at Hamp and he looked at me, still saying nothing. I didn't even get one of his silent statements. The blood had stopped spreading as fast in the gauze but we needed to monitor it closely. I leaned closer and looked into his eyes. "Lay still, bud, I'll be right back."

The limp, unconscious body would have been hard to get up the steps from below even with a normal step riser, but the tall 'gator-proof ones made it a real struggle. It was like lugging a long sack of drywall mud around. I decided the extra bruises and splinters on his backside from a couple of drops wouldn't make much difference so I didn't worry when I lost my grip. He would be going to a place where he would have plenty of time to heal.

After getting him to the top, Byron moved to Pancho Two and started stripping him. He kept worriedly looking over at Hamp.

Hamp hadn't moved while we were gone and the blood had stopped spreading in the gauze bandage. His eyes were still open and they focused on me when I leaned over. "I got shot again, didn't I?"

"Yeah, but the bleeding is about stopped. You probably hit your head pretty hard too. We need to wait a while before moving you just to be safe. Chase went to get help at the east entrance after you got the canoe and should be back any time. The meeting place is at Bugaboo, so we need to go there. You know where you are now, don't you?"

"Canal Run Shelter?"

"Yep. Both bad guys are out cold and By's OK."

"That was a shitty plan, Nobe."

I knew it was coming but I didn't think he would attack that soon in his condition. Annoyed, I said, "No it wasn't. It would have been shitty to not have a plan. From what I could tell, you started out at a sitting position—that had to have slowed you down and made you vulnerable. I don't know what all happened up here, but one guy came sailing through the rail near me into the canal and Byron was pounding the other's lights out when I got up."

Byron looked over his shoulder from his field-stripping. He had the naturally bronze bodies with long raven hair laid out like they were sunbathing on a nude beach. "I sent the guy over the rail because he was closest. The other one was going to shoot me but Hamp yelled when he jumped up and the guy swung and shot him. Hamp still brought him down—I just made sure he was down for the count."

"Jeez, By," I said. "You 'bout killed him."

"I was hitting him easy-like. It was a lot less than he would have done to us, wasn't it?"

Hamp's lips curled dimly. "Maybe it was a pretty good plan after all. I just don't see why I always have to take the bullet every time. I guess I'll have to get a first aid kit like yours. Did you bring it?" He wasn't quite up to speed awareness-wise and that had to include pain, which would be major when he started moving and getting his senses back.

"You're all patched up from it," I said, pointing to the gauze and sling. "Can't leave home without it."

When I left for college Mom and Dad didn't give me a nice book bag or pen set or Day-Planner. They gave me a next-to-the-top-of-the-line first aid kit. Actually, it was called a **medical** kit. I think Mom had to start using a rinse to hide her gray hair in her early thirties because of my tendency to need such care and she said she would be completely gray before Christmas break worrying about me without something to patch up with until someone got me to a doctor. She had a whole shelf in a kitchen cabinet dedicated to the purpose of my repair and it was full of economy-sized boxes and bottles that never lasted past their expiration date when I was at home. I may have the only such kit that has the zipper worn out on it and a nylon handle that came loose at one end. Nothing lasts anymore.

"I'll need some water soon," Hamp said. His voice was beginning to sound husky and trembly. I was glad I had the forethought to bring enough for all of us.

I couldn't help him much without touching near his wound, but he managed to make it to a sitting position by himself and rested his back against a roof support post. I could tell from his face that he was becoming aware of the pain, so I poured out some Advil to wash down. After taking them he shifted his bare back on the post a little and lowered his eyes.

It's hurting like hell, now.

Chapter 15

I was alone operating the fossil-fueled canoe that Hamp stole and Byron was with Hamp in the rental being towed behind me. I tied the connecting rope around their hull with the pulling point under the boat so it wouldn't zigzag so much. The little five-horsepower motor had no problem once we got going and we made good time.

The early morning sky was an opaque pearl gray that cast its dull glow on a shadow-less eerie world without color. Byron had found a cellphone in Pancho Two's pants pocket and I called Jar's dispatcher and told her we were OK and to pass it on to the deputies that would be with Chase by then. I told her Hamp was hurt and she assured me that two county EMTs were with the crew and they were nearing Bugaboo at that time. That was a relief in itself.

We had loaded Hamp into the floor of the trailing canoe and made a backrest out of the Panchos' clothing and the pack, now empty of energy bars and water that we wolfed down after I patched up Byron's knuckles, six of which had the bark peeled off. We cast off under the angry scorched tree canopy that suffered the fiery ball earlier. I felt like I had violated sacred ground by causing such damage in a wildlife sanctuary. The place was a refuge first and a public area second and I hoped our well-being was important enough to justify what I did.

We rounded the last curve before getting even with Bugaboo Island and there they were—a flotilla of boats carrying friendly faces. Standing and waving from one of the two tour barges was the familiar form of Chase wearing a grin. Popper Pearson and Donna Cape, the EMTs, stood next to him and waved me alongside. They had worked on me several different times in years past.

I pulled forward until Hamp's canoe was almost even with them and cut the motor and he drifted into place. He stood on his own and with Byron's and the others' help, he stepped up onto the wide boat and was led to a folding seat. Popper and Donna started to work on him immediately. Alex was nearby on a litter, raised up on his elbows and looking much better than he did last night. He gave a slight wave and I returned it as Byron and I ducked under the canopy to go aboard and accepted the canned drinks that Chase offered when we stood straight. The raised deck had two more litters and an array of medical supplies and containers of implements. Popper and Donna already had Hamp's bloody dressing off and were preparing to clean it again.

"When I told them you were here, they put on extra stuff," Chase said with a grin.

I ignored that. "Where's Jar?"

"On the open tour barge over there with two park rangers and two of his deputies. He and Alex were already on the canal when we got here about twenty minutes ago. They must have heard our motors and came right out to meet us."

I recognized Clement Taber, Jar's deputy, nearby and told him about Hamp's captors being up at the shelter. "They tied up?" he asked.

I glanced at Byron and he was grinning. "They were unconscious when we left, and naked," I said with a straight face.

Donna looked up, smiling. "I'll go!" After no approval, she returned to her work on Hamp, flashing a knowing smile at me.

Sometimes in life, little episodes happen that are remembered in the most unpleasant of ways, like biting your cheek in the same place twice during the same meal. The ingredients for the reminder that flashed through my mind at that moment were me, Donna Cape, and being naked. Even in the midst of a major drug bust, I briefly allowed the flashback some mental air time and tried to keep my face from flushing without success.

Back in my junior year at high school, I was on the football team's second string and spent most of our games holding down the bench, drinking Gatorade, and rubbing my arm across my forehead like it was hard work. I was smaller then and of little use to the team other than being a live practice dummy at workouts. During one particular game we were so far ahead that everybody with a uniform on got to play, including me. The very first play I was in was executed perfectly until a pileup resulted at the end with me near the bottom of it. The referee was nearby and dutifully blew his shrill whistle at the same moment I got kneed in the nuts. The sound blended perfectly with the pain signals in my head. Naturally, Donna Cape was on duty, Popper Pearson being out of town, and I was promptly delivered to her. She was six years older than me but she wore her tailored white blouse well, no bra, and had a pretty, dimpled smiling face like Goldie Hawn. I would have preferred a humane lethal shot of something, but her therapy was direct application of an ice pack. Talk about *cold*.

There I was, a macho guy with broad shoulder pads, narrow hips, a cute butt (so my sister said back then), and hairy legs with my skin-tight pants and jockstrap down to my knees and a little cluster of raisins between my legs. Jeez. Nothing down there came close to resembling what a gladiator such as I should have had. Donna kept thinking it was necessary to check on my condition and readjust the ice pack. Damn, a lot of good that did—cold is cold. I was afraid to look after she discharged me for fear I might have two belly buttons from the withering cold. Why couldn't I have just been shot in the arm by a crazed fan?

"At least you won't have to search them, Clement," someone offered, shaking me from my reverie. There was laughter from several of the nearest boats.

"There's a gun in the canal opposite the broken rail," I remembered. "I doubt you'll find it in the peat, though. Also, the burned-out canoe can be brought back." They just looked at me.

After checking with Jar and the deputy refuge manager, Clement and a Ranger named Dan left in a forest green flat-bottomed powerboat.

I sat on a folding chair near Chase and Alex joined us with his Gatorade, sitting next to me. Byron decided to find the canoe with his extra clothes and change from his pee-spattered ones.

"You don't look like the same person I left a while ago," I said to Alex. "You've got to be feeling better."

"I do. I told Donna the symptoms I had earlier and she said I had heat exhaustion and if you hadn't found and helped me when you did, it could have developed into a heat stroke. I appreciate you helping me, Noble."

It was a heartfelt "thank you" and he looked me in the eye when he said it. It caught me off guard and all I could come up with was, "Nothing to it." We sat quietly a few minutes enjoying the cold drinks.

"Did you and Jar talk any about why you were on the island?" I finally asked Alex. When he came to on the trail after I found him, he was upset over something he had done but he was in no condition to get into it at the time.

"No, Jar had barely recovered from his trip in to uncover the duffel bag when we heard the boat motors. He wanted to get out here and get things moving. What I need to talk about will keep, I guess. They need to go ahead and get the two guys on the island into custody." He stared down at his Gatorade bottle as if he were talking to it.

"What's the plan, Chase?" Byron asked from behind us. He had found his clothes in the canoe on the opposite side of the barge from where we landed and was busy making the change while using us as a shield in case Donna looked our way.

"The deputy refuge manager, ranger supervisor Timothy Tine, and Jar and his captain and lieutenant are working it out," Chase began. "They'll be calling the shots. Randy Taylor, the refuge manager, is letting them handle it. He's at his office at the entrance with some of his office people ready to send us what we need if this is not enough. In the boats, we have all three Rangers, their assistant supervisor, and two equipment operators with handguns in addition to five of Jar's men with their handguns, rifle and shotguns. Greg Conley and two of the four other refuge firefighters are also on the way in case they are needed. Everybody else is helping with the evacuation of the public areas and securing of the entrance.

"Since we are only after two people, and they are pretty much cornered and outnumbered, we all thought it best to take them into custody and then turn them over to the DEA or FBI or whoever wants them—they can fight that out between them. The people here, including us, know the swamp better than outsiders and it would save time having to explain the situation to them, especially to that jerk-off Gus Bunner. It would also lessen the risk of letting the two guys and the drugs slip away. As long as we are set up to keep them from doing that, we might as well nail 'em. When I called Randy and told him what was happening, he didn't hesitate and had everyone assembled within an hour—I was amazed."

"It wouldn't go well if Bunner gets involved," I speculated. "This may be federal land and the drug trafficking is interstate, but there's enough people to clear this up fast without a lot of delay and grandstanding. This whole situation definitely goes beyond the reach of local law officers, considering what we know about Safepoint Security. Jar and Randy Taylor will gladly turn it over to agencies set up for such an investigation, which is apparently already under way by Bunner."

Something I said had caused Alex to stir uncomfortably and he started to say something, but lowered his head again in thought.

Chase continued. "Just about everyone here has a radio and cellphone so communication won't be a problem. As soon as they agree on a plan it should happen quickly. On the way here, Ranger Tine and I discussed that it would be best to close in on the men by land because an approach on open water would definitely be met by gunfire—they would be like sitting ducks. Same thing with a helicopter entry because an automatic weapon could easily bring it down before it was spotted and the fire returned. The Forestry Service is standing by with one, though, just in case."

I watched the refuge air boat bobbing restlessly in the burnt sienna liquid of the canal. It was tied to one of the green boats and must have been towed so the noisy motor and prop wouldn't alert the ones they came for. It could be used to extract the prisoners from the island without herding them through the snarled brush. The fish and wildlife boats and the rentals and tour barges Chase commandeered for the deputies and EMTs were crammed together like Chinese junks. Counting two extra empty canoes, one with a motor, that Chase had brought, the two Jar and Alex paddled out and the two Hamp, Byron and I brought in, there were fifteen water craft stretching across the canal and that same distance lengthwise.

During the lull in the conversation I expected Alex to say what was on his mind, but he didn't. I wondered if he was waiting to talk to me in private. Instead, I said to Chase, "After Byron and I left to find Hamp, Jar was going to dig up the drugs so the couriers could find them and be caught with them. I assume all that went well."

Chase nodded and said, "He went straight to the spot. We talked briefly before they started their meeting and he told me about it. That was a good call because you and Byron stopped the guys with the batteries for the locator. The drugs would never have been found by them without it. The way Jar talked Alex did a good job of hiding them."

Alex took everything in but remained silent. Byron was quiet too, and glanced occasionally over at the progress with Hamp. At varying intervals we all unconsciously tugged at the chigger bites in our groins that refused to go away.

Chase finished his drink and continued. "This will happen fast, I think, and safely too. Randy Taylor has shut down all entrances to this part of the swamp and will get all the canoe parties and campers and fishermen out to be on the safe side. Some of the firefighters and forestry techs are doing that now. Other visitors won't even be let in the gate today, so they don't have to be evacuated. Also, all trail reservations were canceled that included today and tomorrow. Some of Jar's men are guarding the east entrance and the sheriff of Ware County has sealed off the west end at Stephen Foster. No one gets in to help those guys and no one gets out with the drugs."

"Did you stop at Coffee Bay and check on Ty?" I asked. It looked like Byron was not going to ask about him.

"I just slowed down as I passed. I asked if he wanted a ride back to the entrance and he said no. He was fixing breakfast at the time and said he would head on afterwards by himself. He looked clean and rested considering his condition when I left."

Out of the corner of my eye, I noticed Byron's head hang slightly and his shoulders drooped.

"By the way," Chase added, "Mom and Dad got to work soon after I arrived at the rec area and made sandwiches for everybody, so help yourself. There're plenty of drinks too." Chase pointed to coolers in the back of the barge.

Byron and I stood and made a beeline for the food with Chase following close.

Chapter 16

▼

Rather than sit up on the raised deck of the tour boat eating in front of everyone like dogs on leftover biscuits, Chase, Byron and I passed out sandwiches, Little Debbie cakes and drinks to the eager hands in the boats around us. Few in the gathering had had time for breakfast since their call to action was well before wake-up time. Even Jar and the other leaders on the open tour boat accepted the food that Uncle Bob and Aunt Julia had thoughtfully prepared. It looked like their meeting was over and a path was being opened in the cluster of water craft toward its center for briefing of the troops. Hands not holding food or drink slowly pulled the floating command center into position without having to crank motors or drag out paddles.

Tim Tine, the ranger supervisor, was apparently going to lead the expedition and he stood to address us when his boss, deputy refuge manager Bill (Beck) Becker, answered his chirping cellphone. Tim sat back down until he was done.

"Yes, this is Becker." As he listened, his face looked like he had just stepped in a cow pie.

"That's right, Mr. Bunner. We plan to go by land from the upper end of the island—they would least expect that and our men would have more cover.

"Yes, I understand that, but we have plenty of people and we are prepared to move out immediately.…

"An approach by air or water would be awfully exposed. Those men have automatic weap…

"Bunner, I can't help but think about the impact on human life and equipment, not to mention the swamp. I think you are making a mistake. We know the area and can get around better with our experi…

"No, but let me finish just one sentence. There are thirty-five dedicated people that work hard to take care of these 450,000 acres and yes, our worry does enter into it. The sheriff's department counts in this too. This is our home."

I looked around at the faces of the men and women who came willingly on the mission and I saw the high regard for their leader reflected in their faces. Jar and his men looked pleased and smiled at each other in agreement.

Bill Becker was actually second in command to Randy Taylor but he, along with the rangers and equipment operators, carried a firearm and were well qualified and capable of law enforcement. Randy and his office staff usually stayed behind and helped with the logistics of emergency operations as well as many of the normal day-to-day efforts. The arrangement worked particularly well in situations of the magnitude they were prepared to face but they were apparently about to abandon it, through no fault of their own.

Becker was a rangy figure in his mid forties, and his face and mannerisms projected a demeanor of studied calm. He had thin lips and squinting eyes, not from agitation but from serious concentration and understanding of the world around him. He spoke calmly to the FBI agent in a normal voice while a fourth of the total refuge team and a third of Jar's was watching and listening with disbelief and disappointment. Their witness to the conversation would save explanation and time later when they prepared to pull back. They hung on the remainder of Beck's side of the conversation.

"I understand perfectly but I don't like it. I'm sure Randy Taylor is talking with the district office now and I'll be getting my instructions to stand down as soon as we hang up. We have medical technicians here that I will ask to remain along with two guards for their safety. If they agree to stay, they won't interfere and they will remain here on the canal in case they are needed. Also, we already have two men in custody that will be turned over to you when you come by."

Beck stiffened slightly as he listened to Agent Bunner speak.

"No, Agent Bunner, you have refused our help and that includes the dirty work of housing your captives until you are ready to pick them up. I'm sure Sheriff Jarrett's budget doesn't have funds to house criminals in his jail that he won't be prosecuting. You said you have the resources to get the job done, so we need to keep it clean and simple and let you handle the whole operation. Our involvement under the circumstances would just make things more complicated for you and us. The sheriff is on vacation but I'm sure he and his men would agree to suspend their total involvement."

Bill Becker looked at Jar and winked. Jar and his captain were nodding in agreement and grinning. Any compensation the feds might give for their assistance would probably not cover the paper work required to get it and the wait for such funds would be still another matter. Small counties didn't need the expense or aggravation.

"No, it's out of the question. We'll make a clean break of it. Subjecting ourselves to outside orders and conflicting procedures could jeopardize our safety and the protection of the swamp and I ask that you have the same considerations when you make your move. The refuge will be left as you found it. That's no more than we ask of anyone else coming here. When I return to my office I'll fax preliminary information on the capture of the men you will pick up so you can start building your case."

Beck grinned as he listened to Bunner.

"The Secretary of the Interior has considerable control over us. I can give you his number if you like."

Beck pulled the phone from his ear, looked at it, and shrugged—he had been hung up on. A unanimous but quiet ovation sounded from all of us gathered around. It was a perfect opportunity for departments and agencies to work together toward a common goal—each doing what they did best—but upon hearing Beck's side of the conversation, the offer to help Bunner by capturing the intruders was obviously refused with scorn. From what Jar had told about the man on other occasions, I gathered that involvement with someone like him would best be avoided altogether.

I hated to admit it, but under duress, I would have to cast a vote of reluctant tolerance for someone like Special Agent Gus Bunner, even if I disapproved of his methods. He was obviously dedicated, if not gung ho, and come hellfire coals or Polar ice caps he would ride in on some sort of well-bedecked steed, brandishing the latest in swordarm technology, and with his band of merry men, strive valiantly to cage the monsters that the programs and institutions of society have been too slow to overcome. The problem with him was his success rate. If only he would read the how-to manuals first, things might go better for him. Brushing up on his people skills wouldn't hurt either.

Beck's phone rang again before much else was said and I assumed it was Randy Taylor with instructions to withdraw. This time his voice was low and cryptic. After he hung up, he and Jar talked quietly for a while. When they were done, Beck rousted his troops and they headed their fleet back to their compound. In keeping with the irony of the situation, they rode off into the sunrise.

*   *   *   *

Jar had transferred to a flat-bottomed boat with two of his men and let Beck's people take the big tour barge and their armada back to the boat docks. The crowd had been reduced to EMTs Donna and Popper, Hamp, Chase, Alex, Byron and myself on the canopied barge, and Jar and four of his men on the two rental fishing boats. The canoe inventory was left which included two with motors and four without. Deputy Clement and the ranger were still off to Canal Run Shelter to retrieve the naked perps. We all waited for Jar to break the silence. His guarded conversation with Beck before the refuge troops left, and the fact that we were not headed back on their heels, told me that our involvement there was not over.

"Bunner and his people were about ready to leave the launching ramp when he and Beck were on the phone so they should be here in less than an hour. They are coming in three boats, six FBI agents in two of them and three DEA guys in the third. They also have an air boat. They have refused assistance from Beck and my people so legally and politically we have to stay out of it. It's probably for the good because of the confusion and liability involved with so many departments trying to work together under Bunner with little time for planning. Lord knows, Bunner by himself could screw up an anvil.

"The problem is, those guys with all their information, training and equipment are subject to 'misjudgments,' as Beck put it. That's a polite understatement considering things that can go wrong in the swamp. They are thinking about air and water approaches to the lower end of the island and both of those ideas are going to be vulnerable to the gunfire of the men stranded there. With all the cover on Bugaboo, it would be hard to spot their hiding place to return the fire. Boats and 'copters could be shot away like cans on a log. That's the reason I'm asking the medics to stay behind.

"Beck and I thought it would be a good idea to leave a couple of men with a phone and a radio on the island to monitor Bunner's progress and take action if his tail gets in a crack. The medical evac helicopter and an air rescue team in Waycross plus the forestry 'copter have already been put on standby by Randy Taylor. The FBI is operating on a secure channel, so if there were two people on the island and two guards with Popper and Donna here on the barge with communication equipment, we could observe their progress and call for emergency action if they got into trouble. The swamp is still Randy and Beck's responsibility and they need to know what's going on."

"I'll go with you," I told Jar.

"Me too," Chase and Alex chimed in unison. It surprised me that Alex wanted to stay with us but I knew Chase was in for the duration.

"No you're not," Jar said with a frown. "You guys can't be involved in an official police operation. You'll have to go back to the landing." He didn't seem totally committed to what he was saying.

I spoke up promptly to catch the wave. "You can't be involved either, Jar—you said so yourself—but as members of a permitted canoe party on a camping trip, we can all be here; we just happened to have made a wrong turn and ended up on Bugaboo if the question of our being here comes up. The only ones that can officially be here are the guards that Beck said would be left with Popper and Donna."

"And I'll be staying with them," Hamp added.

"Jeez, Hamp—you need to get to the hospital with that arm," Jar said.

Hamp didn't say anything and set his jaw slightly. *I'm shot and I can't be moved. I'm staying.*

"I'll be here with Hamp," Byron said. He was not ready to leave the man that shared in the struggle against the Pancho duo.

Jar pulled out a half-bag of M&M's and munched in concentration while I removed some ticks on my lower legs that were among the chigger bites. I was so numb and preoccupied with all that had been going on, I hadn't seen or felt them. Hamp, Byron and Alex had already gotten theirs along with Donna's help and they had let her wash them with an antiseptic solution. I was a little jealous, especially when Popper started toward me with the bottle and cloth, but with my luck Donna would have used the damned ice pack treatment on my lower-body mites from hell. I graciously accepted the rinse from Popper and did myself, even making a couple of swipes with the moist cloth on the chigger duplex and hi-rise in my pants with the hope that I wouldn't have to scratch down there as much as the other perverts.

After folding the empty chocolate-brown M&M bag and putting it in his pocket, Jar called Clement on the radio and got their status and location. When he finished, he spoke to the rest of us.

"Clement and Dan should be back with the prisoners about the time the feds come by. They have instructions to turn them over to Bunner as they pass on the canal. Those of us going to the island need to be out of sight by then so we should leave in about ten minutes. Ernie, you and Tank stay with the barge with a fishing boat and send them back to the landing after the prisoner transfer so they can share their little experience with the ones that had to go back. They won't be getting back into any kind of routine at the refuge today with all that's going on so they might as well be updated first hand. Snake, you and Red can go ahead on—and not a word to anybody about what we are doing. Noble, you and Chase get some more water and food from the big cooler for us to take to the island but be sure to leave plenty for the ones staying here. Hamp and Byron will remain on the barge for additional medical treatment if anyone asks. Leave one of the portable toilets here too. Alex, help me divide up these firearms and put on a rifle too. We need to keep one of the radios with us and leave the rest here on the barge. We'll use twenty-four as the operating channel but twenty-eight will be the alternate. Clement already gave me my cellphone.

"We'll have a lighter load if we each take a canoe to the island, so divvy up the gear and that will make it easier too. We should take the tents in case it rains. Hamp, offer the two remaining canoes to Bunner if he needs them for shallow water and be sure he gets the prisoners' clothes."

I glanced at Hamp to get his silent reply.
What clothes?

Chapter 17

▼

In addition to the instructions Jar had given us, his plan also included for someone on the first aid barge to notify us on land when Agent Bunner got in sight. Until he arrived, we had some time to set up a temporary camp in the little clearing on the tip of the island. It would provide shelter with the tent flies in place if we needed it and we would have a little comfort while we carried out our watch, which shouldn't last long if Bunner's tactical operation went well.

We were out of view from the canal but by stepping beyond the tree and scrub brush cover we could see with binoculars the part of the canal where the medical boat was moored. We would also be shielded from anyone traveling the meandering water trail to get to the south end of Bugaboo. That was the course going in taken by the men that were stranded and by Hamp when he stranded them going out with their canoe—a course I wondered if Bunner could even find. By walking a short distance to the west side of the camp area, we had a thousand-foot vista of the open prairie that was access to the south end of the island. It included the intersection of the faint trail and the canal at least a mile from where we were. The sight length from the barge wasn't as far and they would be able to see Bunner's entry onto the trail better. At our vantage point, we would only be able to see vague shapes with the binoculars, but from the elevation where we stood on the hammock, the deeper water of the route that must be taken was easily seen. A short walk around some thick foliage revealed another length of the route.

The trip back in to Bugaboo through the shallow water and peat blowups was much easier and faster with one man per canoe and we blasted over and through the vegetation with only one or two stalls. The mid-morning heat was still bearable and our resistance to, or tolerance of, the physical and mental discomfort was also at a higher level.

We were working closely in the small campsite setting up the second tent and I spoke to no one in particular, "I wonder how Bunner got wind of what Safepoint Security has been doing? He must have been watching them for some time to be ready to move in so quickly like this." I looked up, hoping it was a good time to start including Alex in on what we knew had been going on. I was certain by then that he was not involved in the drug operation other than to try to stop it somehow.

Alex looked up from the work he was doing on the tent pegs. "What was that?"

"Bunner, the FBI guy—he's been watching some people that may be involved in the transfer to Georgia of the drugs you found and buried."

"No, I mean the security company—what did you say the name was?"

"Safepoint. Hamp and I were followed by them on the way down here and two men with Safepoint ID broke into his place the night after we got down here. We think they were looking for some incriminating pictures of the drug drop Chase took a few weeks ago. I developed them in my darkroom last week. The charter plane that dropped the duffel is also connected with them."

After the second tent was pitched, Jar, Chase and I situated ourselves in front of the two tents on an extra ground cloth Chase had spread while Alex remained on one knee at the last anchor peg with his other leg poised to get up, his elbow on that knee. He stayed in that position and his stare shifted from me to some unknown point in the distance while he considered what I had said.

Chase saw Alex's look of confusion and disbelief over all that I told him and added, "I wasn't completely honest with you Saturday when I showed you the pictures, Alex. At the time I didn't know who I could trust because somebody knew enough about the pictures I took and wanted them bad enough to keep tabs on Hamp and Noble and break into their place and my camper to look for them. I was pretty sure the only ones I told about them were Mom and Dad and you, but I guess I could have been overheard by someone else."

Nothing was said for a couple of minutes. I was beginning to wonder if it had been the right time to tell Alex all I had or if he really needed to know what I told him at all. It would all be over soon and we would give our statements and be on our way. Jar had not intervened so I took it to mean it would do no harm to let Alex in on what we knew. What I still didn't understand was what triggered Alex to take off by himself and risk his life to intercept the drugs and hide them. I wanted him to trust us and tell us what he knew, but why should he? We hadn't trusted *him*.

"I hope you aren't pissed at me for keeping information from you," Chase said finally. "I guess I got overwhelmed by the way things were building up and I couldn't figure any way to control them other than keeping things quiet and seeing what happened after the canoe trip. I didn't count on ending up in the middle of another drug drop during the trip. This whole mess has had me worried sick and if I hurt you in the process, Alex, I'm sorry."

"There's nothing to be sorry about, Chase. If anybody's withheld information, it's been me. For the past few weeks I've been trying to piece together events and make sense of some of the things that involved me that might be related to some of this drug operation. Now I'm sure I know some things that have a bearing on it, but out of disbelief I've kept quiet about them to see what, if anything, would happen next—just like you. Well, nothing went away and something did happen and I don't think a bag of drugs and four arrests are going to stop or even slow down the group that's doing this. They might miss a week's income but they'll recover. There're too many people involved for them to just abandon ship."

"Do you know any of them?" Jar asked. He had hung on Alex's every word.

"For starters, I know the two at the other end of the island." Alex shifted to a sitting position at the end of the narrow tarp to our left and faced toward the front of us.

"You do?" I asked anxiously.

"John Spanner and Ted Markel. They used to launch their boat every Sunday afternoon at Crooked River State Park and bought junk food, drinks and gas from me at the outfitter where I worked near St. Marys. They claimed they were fishing but they never bought bait or tackle. I helped them just about every time and got to know their names from their charge cards. My boss said they always stayed the night and got back at different times Monday morning. I also learned who they worked for."

"Safepoint Security," Chase guessed.

Alex nodded in agreement. "When Noble mentioned the name on the barge and a while ago I was able to tie some things together."

"Do you know where they went to do their so-called fishing?" Jar asked.

"For a long time they headed toward the ocean but then they started going upriver until five or six weeks ago. I guess they slept on their boat Sunday night. Yesterday was the first time I had seen them in that amount of time."

"Well I'll be darn," Jar said thoughtfully. "Those guys were picking up drugs by way of the river. They must have made a nighttime connection."

"You mean they dropped them from a plane like they did here?" I asked. It actually sounded to me like a better setup than they had been using on Bugaboo Island—at least not as labor intensive with all the paddling.

"Not at night and too public around there in the daytime for that. The timing would have to be too perfect to pick up the goods before somebody else on the river came across them. Unlike the transfer here in the swamp, the swap would have to be direct, as in boat-to-boat.

"The sheriff of Camden County has sent me copies of a lot of information he has received from the Coast Guard concerning their war on drug smuggling, operation 'New Frontier' being one of their latest efforts. Last year they seized close to sixty tons of Colombian cocaine. That's all well and good, but the problem is that amount is only a tenth of the amount that gets through—six hundred tons if you can believe it. That's ninety percent of the cocaine that reaches the United States. Half of that passes through the Caribbean. Since it's U.S. territory, Puerto Rico is a magnet for the Colombian traffickers because shipments from the island to the mainland don't pass through Customs.

"Some of the Coast Guard advisories sent to the coastal towns and counties say that the cocaine is carried in boats called 'Go Fasts.' They are designed for high speed and they're hard to see. If necessary, they'll pull a dark blue tarp over the boat and drift, making them almost invisible to planes or even a ship only a few hundred yards away."

"So when Spanner and Markel headed to big water they could have been picking up a delivery directly from the Go Fast," Alex said with newly dawned interest.

"Exactly. It's more open water and a fast seaworthy boat like that wouldn't attract as much attention as it would coming up the river."

"What about the times they went upstream where the river's more narrow?" Chase asked. "Do you think they dropped the goods from a plane then? The pick-up guys apparently didn't go there to fish."

"I don't think so," Alex replied. "After seeing the plane that made the drop yesterday, I think another plane landed on the water and they transferred the stuff directly from it to the fishing boat."

"How so?" Jar questioned.

"The plane yesterday was white with a green double stripe across the sides. Before Spanner and Markel stopped coming around to the store altogether, I saw a plane with the same markings flying low up the river and it had floats instead of wheels. It could have landed on a remote part of the river and the drugs transferred there. Once, a customer and I saw the plane flying up the river and he said it was a Cessna 185. The one with wheels looked like a Cessna too."

"Hamp said it was a 182," I said. "I think it's more than a coincidence that they are painted the same—the traffickers simply had to change their method of operation from boat to plane delivery because of increased monitoring by the Coast Guard around the Georgia coast and they owned the resources to do it without missing a beat. Then, they changed again to an airplane with wheeled landing gear because it wouldn't attract as much attention. Float gear causes a lot of drag and wasn't needed anyway. By dropping the goods, they wouldn't run the risk of landing in the swamp and hitting a peat blowup or being seen by park personnel."

"I agree," Jar said. "It looks like the pick-ups went from Go Fast boat to float plane and, in the last six weeks, to air drops. The river transfers seem to have stopped around the time I was getting all the information on the suspected smuggling and increased patrols. The Coast Guard must have been giving the area enough coverage to make them change their operation to one more remote. Also, using I-75 for inland transport is probably safer than using I-95 along the coast since the heat was on. I-95 is patrolled more and security around the submarine base near it is tight anyway. They are obviously flexible enough to change their operation quickly to one with the least risk and rely on intelligence gathered by Safepoint to trigger the changes."

All four of us jumped when Byron's tinny drawl came on the radio.

"Hey! Y'all hear me?"

"Loud and clear, good buddy," I came back. "Do you copy?" I didn't know the latest radio procedure but figured what I had picked up from old movies and TV reruns was better than Byron's style. I was pretty sure he was supposed to say, "Come in, Mother Hen," or "Breaker one-nine,"—or "Breaker two-four" in our case—but I didn't want to be a smart-ass. There are proper ways to do almost everything, especially in law enforcement.

"What?"

"Can you hear me?"

"Sure."

"Go ahead." I wished he'd let one of the county people use the radio.

"Clement and Dan just came in sight from getting the Panchos and I guess it's the Bunner patrol I see coming from the other way."

"Looks like show time," Jar said as he pulled a box of Milk Duds from a cooler.

Chapter 18

The sun was still on its climb in a cloudless sky and the degrees of air temperature increased in direct proportion with the degrees of the angle of its rays. Without morning cloud cover, heat got an early start in the Southeast throughout the year. The sparse population and lack of polluting industries near that part of the Georgia coast made the sun's work easy to get through the earth's atmosphere to the back of our neck.

The swamp teemed with the activity of air, ground and water creatures with plans to complete their morning chores so they could spend the hot part of the early April day seeking cool breezes and shady places. Wading bird rookeries were active and the golden-orange prothonotary warblers flitted about singing their sweet-sweet-sweet songs. Sandhill crane chicks were beginning to hatch that time of year and ospreys could be seen taking food to their young in bulky nests high in lonely pines. Bull alligators bellowed warnings to others of his territorial boundaries and mating duties.

On that day, however, the peaceful scene was slowly being profaned by the increasing hum, whine and roar of outboard and air boat motors on the canal....

...and by Byron's etiquette-less radio voice.

"Hot damn! Look at those fucking boats!"

Even in the sober times we faced, Jar, Chase and Alex broke into uncontrolled laughter.

I was miffed. There I was about to witness a major drug bust and in my hand was an official piece of communication equipment erupting in profanity and lack of protocol. I was determined to maintain my proper manner and said, "That's a ten-Roger, Unit Two. What's your observation?" Damned if he was going to be Unit One with his behavior.

"Huh?"

"What do you see?"

"Why can't we be Unit One? We've got more people."

Jeez. "Because Jar is here and he's the leader so we are Unit One, shithook. Now, what the fuck is going on?" The majority of Unit One was still roaring with laughter and I was getting a headache.

It took a moment but Byron regained his enthusiasm. "Those are the prettiest boats I've ever seen, guys—three wide, shallow draft beauties that look a little like well-equipped fishing boats but they are painted deep blue with big yellow FBI letters on the side. There're nine men, all with guns, in the boats—six with FBI Windbreakers and caps and three with DEA stuff on. A blue air boat is bringing up the rear with two more FBI guys. Man, what a sight! They're gonna kick some felonious butts."

Byron's voice was starting to be drowned out by the noise of the motorized fleet and the din we heard increased greatly even without hearing it on the radio. "Guys, I'm going to hang up a minute so we can give them the canoes and Pancho clothes—it's getting too loud around here to talk anyway."

"Roger that," I replied.

"Huh?"

"Never mind."

* * * *

We eagerly stepped around to the point where we could see the awesome sight Byron had just described. They would come into view off to our right just before they got to Unit Two's barge, so we could watch the transfer of clothes and canoes, if they wanted them, to the feds' boats.

"There's Clement and Dan in the ranger boat," Jar said, pointing to the left limit of our view. "They're just in time to turn over the prisoners before Bunner's crew gets busy picking up the other two and should get to the barge by the time the clothes and canoes are picked up."

We returned our gaze to the barge and stood speechless as Bunner's forces passed it without slowing. The deputies, EMTs and Byron were waving wildly to get them to stop while Hamp stood watching, probably with a grin on his face. The feds stopped well beyond the barge when they got even with the ranger boat because it wouldn't give way but Jar had the binoculars and had to tell us what was going on.

"Bunner must be highly pissed. I can't see facial expressions but his body language is pretty clear. His arms are going every which way and he's pacing back and forth on the deck. Now he's shaking his fist at the barge, toward the island and at Clement and Dan. Clement's started with the pointing and shaking of fist and…yep, there goes Dan. Some of the feds have lit up smokes and are watching something across the canal. Five bucks says Bunner gets the prisoners, naked or not. Clement would turn over Cameron Diaz if he was told to."

We didn't take Jar up on that because we knew of his deputy's dedication.

"There they go," Jar said proudly after a moment. "Clement's helping the naked guys change boats. Bunner's flinging his arms at his men now and they have turned their attention to their captives."

"Transfer complete," Clement said on the radio. I swapped our radio for the binoculars so Jar could acknowledge him.

"Four," Jar said simply. Damn, that was smooth. It was also shorter than saying ten-four or ten-Roger and it was anonymous.

We watched as Clement and Dan moved away from the G-men and traveled the quarter-mile down the canal to the barge. They would likely get some refreshment and practice telling their tale to Unit Two before heading to the recreation area to spin their yarns there. I was surprised that Jar didn't get the details from them by cellphone, but he must have gotten enough from the flailing arms to satisfy him until the story was told and retold with embellishments in the months to come. My headache was getting better since I hadn't used the radio for a while, so I decided to wait and get the full conversation when we returned, which shouldn't be more than an hour or two, assuming the plan to reach the island by air or water would work.

Bunner decided to transfer the naked men back to the DEA boat, probably so he wouldn't have to conduct the invasion while having male genitals constantly in view. Wars have probably been lost with less distraction. After the switch, he appeared to give more instructions to his men and they all headed up the canal in the original order toward the turn-off to go to the lower end of the island. They were proceeding slower, presumably so they could see the faint water trail they needed to take, but at their rate of progress it would still take ten or fifteen minutes to get there if they chose the way Hamp came out on. I saw Bunner refer to something when he was briefing his men so he must have gotten a detailed Fish and Wildlife survey map, though I doubted the route he wanted showed on it. All but the most defined trails and land mass changed frequently due to peat blowups and large shifting clumps of vegetation. Many areas that appeared to be solid land was so unstable that you could make tall trees and bushes tremble by stomping on it. When we went on a high school class trip to Washington, I saw old maps in the Library of Congress dating from as far back as 1790 with six spelling variations of Okefenokee, but they all basically came from "Ecunnau" meaning earth, and "finocau" meaning quivering, making up the Indian word for "Quivering Earth." I got an

"A" out of Mrs. Evers, and rightfully so, for a twenty-page report I got Mom to type for me that I wrote mostly from info gathered from that trip and talking to my real-life source of older Stones. It also redeemed me for getting caught on the trip by "Never-Evers" in the basement of those hallowed halls feeling up Amy Marshell. I still get that lower spasm when I think about the trouble I could have been in if she had turned me in.

* * * *

We were back sitting on the ground covers in the weak shade of pine trees having another snack and sipping water when Jar asked Alex, "Those guys they're fixing to pick up—Spanner and Markel—are they the only ones you know involved in all this?"

Alex started looking uncomfortable again and hesitated like he was forming words in his mind. Before he finished the first sentence with his brother's name in it, the words hit me like a hammer.

"At the reunion, Tucker started asking questions about the pictures Chase took of the plane. I asked him how he knew about them and why he was interested and he said Dad mentioned them and he was just curious about it. I didn't tell him much because I didn't know much. Chase had told me the day before that there was probably nothing to the flights into the swamp and the pictures he showed me were too blurred to reveal anything, so that's what I told Tucker. His sudden interest in the swamp and what I knew made me start to wonder about him."

"Did you get the blurred prints out of the trash can Saturday?" I asked. I knew it had to be him.

Alex nodded. "I got them because I was tired of all the questions about the plane and pictures and was hoping they would put an end to them. By that time, I was having strong suspicions of something illegal going on and felt like I was being pumped to find out what anybody knew at the east entrance. I wanted to turn the pictures over to see if the curiosity ended after seeing them."

Chase picked up on that. "But that was Saturday—Tucker didn't get here until late Sunday morning. How did you know he would be asking questions? Did he call you from Atlanta?"

"I didn't get the pictures to show Tucker. I got them to show Dad."

Chapter 19

We were all shocked at Alex's statement. Grady apparently had been quizzing him for information and passing it on to someone. That someone must have been Tucker since he was asking about the pictures too. We waited for Alex to continue because we needed to know if and how his dad and stepbrother fit in with the drug transfers and who they answered to, if anyone.

"Before you ask me why I haven't said anything before now," Alex said, "it's because I didn't know anything concrete. For the last month or so, Dad would ask me about work and I welcomed it because we seldom talked. He would ask about the refuge workers and what they did each day, and he was very interested in what I knew about the plane flying over Bugaboo and especially about the pictures you took, Chase. I started making it a point of being aware of what was going on by asking questions and keeping my eyes open so we would have something to talk about in the evenings. I was actually naïve enough to think we were becoming closer."

"What about Charlene Luther?" I asked. "She was with you Saturday night but she left with Tucker after the fight Sunday."

"She works with Tucker and was supposedly passing through from a business trip in Jacksonville and was staying over at the Days Inn to go back with him Sunday night. He asked me to take her to the party so she would have something to do. You probably noticed she was all over me, but it was obvious that she was just after the same information Dad and Tucker was. She kept asking about Noble's hobby developing pictures and Chase's hobby taking them and it wasn't out of casual interest—she wanted information. I was so fed up with her that I took her back to the motel in Folkston without earning or collecting her 'reward.' I made up my mind to head into the swamp and see if there was another Monday flight over Bugaboo—all the interest and questions seemed to point to that. When Noble mentioned Safepoint Security, I remembered the guys here on the island worked for them, so that just doubled my suspicions that something was going on. To tie that name in farther, I realized Tucker's company in the Atlanta/Athens area is Transpoint Couriers."

Chase and I exchanged glances when Jar added, "When I checked on the plane in Key West, it was under the name of Southpoint Charter. Coincidence with the similarity in names? I don't think so."

"Why did you and Tucker fight?" I asked.

"It started out as a verbal argument when I questioned him about his sudden interest in what was going on here in the swamp. He never gave a shit about anything or anyone south of Atlanta since he left for college seven years ago—anyone except Dad, that is, and I think that was a money thing. They communicated frequently either by phone or e-mail, which was far more contact than Dad and I had. He was usually in bed when I got in from work and if not, he holed up in his office with the door closed. Dad had helped Tucker get started in the courier business with heavy investment of his insurance settlement money from the wreck he and Reba were in so I guessed he was still involved with the business in some way. Tucker has his bookkeeper send a check for Dad's phone and Internet bill and I get a little rent money for the use of a bedroom for his office space that he deducts on taxes."

"You own the place in St. Mary's? I thought Grady owned it." Jar wondered.

"He does. It's been in only Dad's name since Mother died four years ago. He took out a mortgage with me cosigning while waiting on slow insurance money but I pay the mortgage note and the utilities. His disability check mostly goes for doctor bills and expensive medicine for pain since his insurance has long since played out."

"What caused the argument to come to blows?" I asked.

"Tucker told me that Dad had decided to sell the home place and move to Miami and help start up a courier service branch there. He said Dad would be close to a medical group that had made great advances with his type of paralysis in its treatment and rehabilitation. I knew better. Dad had been to the best doctors in Albany, Macon and Atlanta, and the surgery he had and the drugs he's on are all they can do for him. Tucker is just using that treatment bullshit to get the proceeds from our home to go into his business, which apparently is drug related."

"Why can't he just use his drug money?" Chase asked. "There's bound to be big money in that. In fact, there's seven digit incentive right here on Bugaboo to expand their horizons."

"That's the trouble," Jar said. "It's big money all right, but it takes time and care to process and distribute the drugs and launder the proceeds into the system. With a lot of hands out for their share, clean money could be hard to come by—especially if they wanted to expand. The amount of cash outlay for a Transpoint branch in Miami is much easier to explain if it comes from someone like Grady investing the proceeds of the sale of his farm or of his insurance settlement. If Tucker is involved in the drug transfers, which I think we can all agree on, he's bound to have money, but it is probably in safe deposit boxes or other hiding places waiting its turn to show up in accounting books legally. Even so, much of that goes toward a lifestyle he has probably come to know and love, judging by the car he drives and the way he dresses."

It was already after the noon hour and the curtain was yet to open on Bunner's show. The performers had to be hot in the sun's blaze but the last time we looked, there was no hint that the raid was about to start. If he was as big a screw-up as Jar let on, maybe he was operating well on the side of caution. We knew we might as well save our energy and stay in the shade and drink plenty of liquids. While we waited, Alex continued his answer to my question about why they fought.

"Tucker said they already had a buyer for our place including the furnishings and that the closing was set up for today at two o'clock. He said I had two weeks after that to get myself and my personal belongings out. I asked why the hell I wasn't consulted and given an opportunity to buy the place and he said I would never have been able to swing a loan that big. He said they didn't have the time for me to apply for one anyway. Like a fool, I just started punching and got in a couple of lucky swings before he whipped my ass. I couldn't help losing my temper—even with someone so much bigger and stronger. To think that Dad got suckered in by his stepson and left his own flesh and blood out of the plans is something I'll never understand. When the rest of the family finds out the place was sold to outsiders, there's going to be a major fuss."

"Do you think he could have been forced in some way to sell like that?" Chase asked. "Maybe they threatened harm to him or you if he didn't sell."

"He could have, or he might have been fooled with the false hope of some medical breakthrough for his paralysis. Whatever the reason, the place is sold now and there's no backing out at this point without penalties I couldn't afford to pay. I doubt seriously that Dad will see any of the money anyway. His insurance money got pissed away awful fast when Tucker started the courier service in Atlanta."

"I can't believe he did it without telling you before now," I said. "The sales contract was probably signed at least a month ago for the closing to be so soon. Even a cash real estate deal takes time to set up with the title search and all. Did you talk to Grady about him selling out without talking to you?"

"I asked him about it Sunday when I took him home and he said it was his place and he could sell it if he wanted to. He made it clear that he still had a life in spite of his disability and he could live his and I could live mine and we could do it without living together in that house. I hurt so bad physically from my fight with Tucker and my argument with Dad hurt even more mentally so I gave up and went to bed. In spite of not being able to do anything about the situation, I was determined to find out what I could yesterday, hoping it would shed some light on Tucker's motivation and Dad's behavior. I had to find out something, and what I've learned has definitely been an eye-opener up to this point. Hell, guys, I took care of him the best I could for the two years since the accident and he treats me like I'm not even his son. How could he shut me out like that? I was there for *him*."

I didn't think Alex expected an answer from Jar, Chase or me. It was just a repeat of an unanswered question he said he confronted his dad with Sunday. Alex's voice was weak and almost broke when he finished. He cleared his throat as if to show that that was causing the strain in his voice. I sensed his defeat and ached so for him and I knew that Jar and Chase did too. At that point I had no idea what to do. We were all hot and tired and at the moment, stuck on Bugaboo Island and the reason was no longer clear or meaningful, other than to witness Gus Bunner's siege and capture of Spanner and Markel. Surely with his resources he could pull it off without us observing, but Becker wanted us there. After Alex's story about his dad and stepbrother and the old home place being sold, I was sick of the whole ugly situation and in no mood for excitement or adventure. Any form of justice that might prevail after the capture we were about to witness had little meaning in the grand scheme of things because taking into custody a total of four minor players of even the smallest of drug rings could hardly be called a victory. To have the bond of kinship loosen was a worse defeat for us.

I didn't even want to talk about it any more but Jar broke the silence.

"Do you really think Tucker is going to care for Grady in Miami?" he asked no one in particular.

A full minute passed before Alex answered.

"No, I don't. Dad can do a lot of things for himself, including driving his special-rigged van, but he relied on me for convenience. Tucker has no idea what Dad's needs are or how to help him. Even if he did, he won't have the time to bother with him while starting up a new business. He'll end up putting him in an assisted-care home and forgetting him. That's looking at it on the positive side—slums are full of abandoned parents." Alex's voice was stronger and he spoke with resolve, but I could tell he was fed up and ready to go.

"Places that care for people like that are expensive," Jar said. "If Tucker gets control of the money from the sale, I doubt if Grady will benefit from any of it."

"What do you mean, Jar?" Chase asked with a concerned look. "He has special needs and it will take money to see that they are met. Miami is not the cheapest place to live—disability or not."

Jar said, "I'm wondering if Tucker is really going to take Grady with him."

"There's been no mention of other arrangements," Alex said. "They were going to Miami after the closing today so I assumed they would look for a place to stay. I'm not so sure, now. He thought a moment. "You think he's in danger, don't you?"

"Him, and possibly you too."

Chapter 20

▼

The sound of distant thunder marked Jar's words with foreboding. Another afternoon storm was coming up and the sinister rumble matched our situation and mood perfectly. We sat helpless, waiting on Gus Bunner to put his plan into action while thoughts took over my mind of Alex losing his home and father with no say in the matter. I hesitated to believe that their lives could be at risk like Jar suggested, but any hindrance to an operation with such financial potential would surely be dealt with as a threat. A funneling of effort or funds that were not directly related to smooth performance of their work would be a liability to be eliminated—a goal for any business. Limited to a wheelchair, Grady's usefulness beyond the proceeds from selling his place was starting to look minimal.

The next thunderous rumble sounded much closer than the last and well ahead of the rounded mass of cumulus clouds that were preceding the afternoon's storm. The others noticed the abrupt skip in distance too and we all looked to the west toward Billy's Island. The rumble turned into a deep chattering roar as its source appeared over the wooded land area in the form of a dark military-type helicopter moving fast toward the opposite end of Bugaboo from us.

"Hot damn! Here comes Rambo! You guys see this shit?" Airwaves from hell were back to haunt me and I wanted no part of it. Jar picked up the radio and acknowledged.

"That's the Feebs finally making their move. Now we'll see if the air approach works."

Bunner had moved the shallow-draft boats about two hundred yards from the canal into the faint trail toward the end of the island but had stopped there. That was probably as far as they would go because of their width and they were likely grounded. I noticed movement on the blue air boat and it started advancing from the rear at a steadily increasing speed. In addition to the FBI man on the driver's platform and another up front, he had picked up two more men, making it three people filling the cramped space in the hull at the front of the boat. Along with the increasing speed, the propellers built up strong wind currents that blew back a heavy wet spray that likely included leaves, stems and small branches of swamp vegetation. The acceleration was fast and it swung around the three stranded boats, losing them in the heavily jetted mist behind it. Bunner was going for an air and water approach.

The clattering, thumping noises of propellers on the airborne and waterborne craft blended together as they slammed the air for the motion required of them and their sound, even at their distance from us, drummed across the wet prairie into my ears as if any second I would feel the backwash from the blades. Both were about a mile away and as close to us as they would get on their way toward the far end of the island.

I watched the animated mayhem on the government boats behind the accelerating air boat as the stinging spray cleared in its wake. Most of the feds were prone on the boat decks in reaction to the deluge while others were already on their hands and knees, recovering from the trashy blast. Two men either took shelter in the water or were blown in and were clamoring to get back on board. I could imagine the cursing from them and Gus Bunner after the unscheduled swamp bath.

Not long after the 'copter completed its low flight over the trees of Billy's Island, the fast-approaching thunderclouds dumped its gray screen of heavy rain to block sight of the land mass and in another minute it would hide Honey Island farther to the south in the same way. The sun was still shining on us but within ten minutes the dark wall of water would close in on Bunner's men and, not long after, us on Bugaboo and I was thankful we had the two tents set up for shelter. Even with a peaceful surrender from the drug men, their capture would have a wet ending. Talk about bad timing.

We didn't anticipate resistance from Spanner and Markel. A valiant stand by them would be fruitless against such overwhelming odds. From their end of the island they could see Bunner's four water craft, one of which was headed their way, and the threatening black chopper was bound to strike fear in their hearts. The chance of rescue by one of their own was nil at that point because the Panchos had been waylaid and communication with them cut off. If they still had contact with an accomplice at the east or west entrances, they would know that the swamp was sealed off with no exit possible. Only fools would offer resistance.

Then we heard the metered pop of automatic weapons joining the racket of the invasion.

*　　*　　*　　*

We were at the last point of our camp area with a sight opening through the foliage and we could barely see the end of the island where the boat landing would take place. The clearing where the rotted cabin site was could not be seen but it was the likely landing place for the 'copter, which was a thousand feet from its goal. The air boat was about twice that distance from the shore.

The gunfire came from the island and I couldn't determine the target until I saw a dark vapor spray from the upper part of the helicopter and then a puff of black smoke came from the same area. The 'copter yawed involuntarily several times, then banked to the left and headed toward the canal parallel to the island but at an increased distance from it. Moments after it changed direction, the air boat spun around in a tight half-circle and began retracing its path. After a quarter mile the 'copter's engine noise and rotor thump changed drastically and it looked doubtful they would make it to the canal. Blue-black fumes continued to pour from the engine area but the flight still appeared under control. We followed its smoky path until it was within a mile of the canal and the power plant reluctantly started coughing to a halt. As it did, the pilot stopped forward motion and quickly lowered them the two hundred feet to the swamp. Following the foamy splash, it sank into the water and soft peat bottom until half the wide troop and cargo door midway of the craft was submerged. It tilted slowly forward in the mush until the four rotor blades barely reached the water and the remaining revolutions caused a wet cylinder of spray to engulf the chopper and rebound upward and continue to swallow it in a drenching cloud like mist from a giant atomizer. The tail stabilizer remained high and dry.

The air boat veered from its original route of retreat and skimmed through aquatic plants and brown silken water toward the stricken chopper, which had landed halfway between our end of the island and the remainder of Bunner's men. It was still a mile from the canal.

If the first aid crew were a half-mile farther north on the canal, they would be closer to the crippled craft but could gain access to it only by the canoes they had, and even then with great difficulty. I mentioned it to Jar and he picked up the radio to give instructions to his men.

"Ernie, come in."

"Go ahead."

"You and Tank take the barge up the canal a ways to be closer to the crash site. If the guys on the air boat look like they are having trouble with the rescue, you may have to paddle the canoes in to help them. Wait for them to wave you in, though, because it's a tough trip with no trail. If there are bad casualties, the evac chopper may want to get them from the air with a cage when the storm passes.

"Did you copy that, Evac?"

"Ten-four, Sheriff. We are available and are monitoring you and Special Agent Bunner's secure channel and can relay messages to your EMTs if they are needed. We are aloft between them and the east entrance but will have to go back and land soon because of the weather coming in. Holler if you need us. Med-Evac 304, standing by."

"Four," Jar said. "You with us on that, Beck? 'Copter's down but it hit easy. Can't tell about casualties."

"I'm hearing but not wanting to. Hope you can get out of the rain. We'll figure out something after it passes."

By the time the air boat reached the downed chopper crew, the door was already open and two men were on top training extinguishers into the steaming engine compartment on the unseen source of the darker smoke. Two others stood in the partially submerged doorway but it was too far away to tell if they were injured.

The rounded dark mountains of thunderheads pushed toward us ahead of a wide apron of consuming rain, and frequent lightning and thunder marked its progress with bright and loud warnings. Bunner's three outboard boats would soon be hidden by the downpour and not long after, the rescue efforts would be hindered or stopped.

Then us. We started making our way to the tents. There would be a chilly down-draft first and the rain would be on us within ten minutes.

"Fuck this shit. Let's just go on in and get Spanner and Markel and get this farce over with. I need to get back and turn Dad and Tucker in and start packing and looking for a place to live."

Alex's profound statement surprised us all. His willingness to attempt the capture of two heavily armed men was a shock in itself, but the problems he faced when he returned home, when stated so simply, hit me like a brick. His brother was involved in a major drug ring and his dad was obviously an accomplice, so they had to be stopped and punished. The house he was born and raised in was sold out from under him and he had to be out in two weeks. With such major decisions and changes coming up, I could understand that confronting two thugs was just part of the shit slung at him and he was ready to meet it all head-on. At least with the four of us there was some control over the outcome if we planned it right.

"He's right, guys," I said. "This whole thing has been slowly getting out of control, especially for Alex. There's a lot on him right now and if we can get these two men under control, it's a step in the right direction. Bunner's relying too much on things with motors to grab them. Let's head toward their end and take them during the storm while their guard is down."

Without a word, Chase went to a canoe and grabbed a coil of rope he was famous for on camping trips. I guessed it was for tying up instead of tying down. Jar was close behind, retrieving the guns his men brought from the department's arsenal and loading all four of them. Alex and I filled two small packs with snacks and bottled water and Chase put my medical kit and extra ammunition in his. We all wore tee shirts and shorts and since it was so hot we stayed with that rather than mess with the hot restricting rain gear. Our caps would keep most of the rain out of our faces.

As Jar passed out the holstered weapons, he said, "Fellas, ya'll should already know how to use these. Since we don't have belts, you'll have to carry them or put them in your waistband. Let's get as far as we can before the storm gets here. We'll scope things out when we get to the burial mounds and see what we need to do. They may seek shelter in the oaks so keep a lookout when we get near them." He turned off the cellphone and radio so a call wouldn't give us away when we got closer to Spanner and Markel and placed them in the pockets of his cargo shorts and buttoned the flaps.

Jar didn't lecture us or tell us to be careful with the revolvers. On many of our get-togethers Jar would sign out for some .38 Caliber Smith & Wesson Police Positives and 7mm rifles from the sheriff's department armory and we target practiced for hours in a remote field near Mom and Dad's. Alex went with us if he could and when he did he was still better than all of us, including Jar. I had also heard he went target shooting on some of his days off with Buddy Brant, the gun collector, so he should be pretty good. He had a natural ability with a firearm, his concentration and determination unwavering, even with an unfamiliar weapon. If he was able to fire off an initial three-shot grouping on a target, he then became one with the piece.

We ducked into the jungle without considering which path was best because we found out earlier that there was no easy one. The primal unfriendly place resisted our passage as it did before but our determination restored us and drove us on without complaint.

* * * *

We were a half-mile through the dense maze when the thunderstorm reached us. Huge drops pounded and soaked the vegetation above us, lowering our headroom and making us bend lower as we ran the green gauntlet. High winds slammed the raw vines, briars and sharp fronds on each side like rapiers and cutlasses into our arms and sides. We felt none of it as the drenching rain rinsed and cooled the burn of muscles and sting of skin. We were so pumped we had to force ourselves to slow down when we neared the openness of the oak grove midway of the island. The chance to stand upright for more than a few seconds sent waves of relief over our neck, back and stomach muscles.

We proceeded with caution to the spot where Jar dug up the duffel of drugs for Spanner and Markel to find. It was missing, so they had taken the bait; we would catch them with the goods. Jar needed to rest a minute, and thankful for the chance to catch our breath, we all huddled under a giant oak to hear his plan.

"They must have carried it to the place where they landed to wait on their rescue," Jar said of the missing bag. He had to speak up above the pounding rain. "Let's head that way but still be on the lookout among the oaks in case they came back this way for shelter from the storm. The element of surprise will still be on our side."

"Wait a minute, guys. I think we might have messed up." Chase had his cap off and spattered rain that flowed down his tense face as he spoke. Ever the worrier, he often came across in a negative way like Jar and his natural logic. "Since Bunner's attack, these fellas know they are not safe for long on this end of the island and they've surely given up on being picked up in canoes by the Panchos. Wouldn't it make sense for them to seek shelter in the thicket or even make their way toward the canal to be picked up there? They may not realize the swamp is sealed off, but they'll try anything they can to buy a little time and hope for rescue."

"He's got a point," Alex offered. "Remember, they have the phone and are in contact with the outside world so they might still try to get the drugs out. With so much a stake, they would be ready to try anything."

"Could they get the duffel through the thicket?" I asked. "It's a heavy load to carry in a crouch even for two people."

"There are two smaller dry bags in the big one," Alex said. "I had to separate them because of the weight and make two trips when I brought them here to hide; then I returned them to the big bag."

Something occurred to me and a sinking feeling went along with it. "If the bad guys are headed toward our camp, there're four canoes to choose from to get to the canal and the barge is no longer there to block their exit. They could hit the canal and head toward the east entrance with no problem."

"That's as far as they would get, though," Jar said. "Bill Becker will have that end sewed up tight. We could follow at a distance to keep the squeeze on them and Beck can nail them when they dock.

"Just to be sure they are headed that way, let's make our way to where they first came on the island and if they aren't there, we can head back to the camp and see if they got one of the canoes."

The rain slackened some but continued to pelt us as we headed to the place where Hamp had snatched the canoe. There would be no need to check beyond that point because there was no decent access to the island anywhere else on that end. I tried not to lower my guard in case the men were ahead of us, but I was satisfied they had left the sparse cover of the pines and went to the north end of Bugaboo where we were set up.

We found the big dry bag and it was empty. They had split up the load to make travel easier.

"My fault, guys," Alex said with a long face. "If I hadn't got so impatient, we wouldn't have made this trip and they would have come straight to us."

"Yeah, and come up on us and started shooting," Jar said. "Leaving camp probably saved our lives—it's easier to pull out a few ticks than a few bullets.

"Let's go on back. They are probably at the canoes by now but be on the lookout in case we catch up with them. We can break camp right quick and meet Byron at the canal and follow them in to the landing."

Jar radioed Deputy Manager Bill Becker at the east entrance to explain the situation and warn him to be ready for two visitors in a canoe headed his way. Then he called Ernie, his deputy on the first aid barge, and asked for an update on the shooting of the chopper. Ernie replied that Donna and Popper would soon be done patching cuts and scrapes on the helicopter crew. He said no one knew Bunner's next move other than to get their fancy boats unstuck. The Med-Evac pilot had relayed the word that Spanner and Markel were no longer on the island so Bunner would probably be joining the 'copter and air boat crews at the barge to plan their withdrawal.

Jar told him and Tank to stay there in case they were needed and to have Byron gas up the outboard motors on the confiscated canoe and the one that Chase brought and meet us with them where our trail met the canal. We would soon leave Bugaboo behind and it would be in style.

Chapter 21

▼

The rain finally stopped during our return trip to camp. I was surprised to find the remaining three canoes unharmed, but in their haste, Spanner and Markel must have thought there was little threat in a few campers and they were probably glad no one was around to slow them down. I was glad we weren't there to be shot at. We hurriedly struck the tents and loaded the few items that were laying around so we wouldn't have to return for them later. Luckily we didn't set up a typical camp because the chore would have taken two hours the way we normally scatter things. By the time the four of us struggled to the canal in only three canoes, Byron was waiting for us in a motorized canoe with his driving finger flipped upward, his cap turned sideways and a stupid grin on his face, and Hamp was bent over in the other one mooning us. Damn, it was good to get back to civilization.

Hamp assured us he was OK and wanted to get on back and Byron agreed. They were fed up with the progress toward capturing the bad guys too. It was getting crowded on the barge and would be even more so when Bunner's three boatfulls got there to raid the coolers and cast blame at one another. As we tied the rental canoes to the powered ones with Chase's unending supply of rope, I told Hamp and Byron about our fruitless trip to the end of the island, but how it possibly saved us from being caught off guard when Spanner and Markel came through with the drugs. We were all relieved that the bad guys were headed for certain capture.

Or were they?

Jar, on the other hand, was still wary. He made sure that all of us, except Hamp with his shoulder wound, had a revolver handy and that the loaded rifle was within Alex's reach. In addition to the critical way he looked at most things, his cautious nature made him come across as unnecessarily negative, but we usually went along with him. My thoughts at that moment was getting back to terra firma and seeing if life was any friendlier there.

Alex was the designated sharpshooter, rifle or handgun, and was assigned to the front of the lead canoe. He leaned his elbows on the camping gear behind him to keep watch on the flat water ahead. Jar was at the controls of the motor while Chase lounged against a pack in the trailing boat. I was in the middle canoe of the three being pulled by Byron with my feet propped on the thwart in front of me while my back rested in the fork of the stern. Hamp sat erect, as always, in the bow in front of Byron. The third canoe in our train had only camping gear in it and brought up the rear. It was good to be making progress on the water without having to do it with paddles.

As it did the day before, the sun came out after the storm to make up for time lost and the humidity baking out of the swamp continued to soak the oily wet film on our skin and fill our lungs as if we were breathing water. What little breeze stirring from our forward motion gave some relief from the swelter but no more could be asked from the little five-horsepower motors.

There was no sign of Ty as we neared Coffee Bay Shelter but there were signs of him being there. The empty cans and wrappers stood out like banners in the natural setting. Jar pulled next to the bank while Chase stepped out with a plastic bag to pick up the trash. There was no room for our three-part tandem rig at the bank behind theirs, so we eased alongside them and Byron stepped across their lead canoe and quietly helped with the cleanup of his brother's thoughtless mess. Ty had planned to head back to the recreation area after breakfast, so he should have gotten there well before the storm and was probably clean, cool and rested. We had five miles to go before getting serious with those comforts, but they would be easy ones.

* * * *

Even after breaking camp on Bugaboo and stopping briefly at Coffee Bay, we expected to catch up with Spanner and Markel and we did. Though at half-speed to save gas, the little outboards on the square-stern canoes churned us along the tannic water over twice as fast as the paddlers. Our goal was not to reach them, however, but with our presence, to eliminate the option of them turning back once they realized they were heading into a trap. We were tired of the chase and had little interest in taking part in the capture other than to get them out of circulation.

As we rounded a slow bend in the canal, Alex suddenly sat erect and that was enough to alert the rest of us. We each, in turn, got a view of the straight-away ahead as we plowed forward and spotted the fleeing canoe about a half-mile or more ahead, only it didn't seem to be fleeing. It was crossways of the canal and was not moving. We could make out the forms of Spanner and Markel through the thick humid air but not what they were doing—not until we noticed circular rippling of the still water ahead of us and the delayed report of an automatic weapon. There was no tight cluster of spraying bullets but, instead, random small splashes at least one hundred feet apart in any direction. At that distance, the slightest movement of the shooter or any tiny variance in wind or makeup of the bullets could cause the slugs to land over several acres. Jar and Byron still shut the motors down and we drifted to a stop. None of the shots reached us but we weren't sure if increasing the angle of trajectory would give them more range. There was no sense in taking chances so we held our position. Some of the bursts of fire came a minute or two apart, so more than likely, they were warning shots and we saw no reason not to heed them.

"Fire a few shots their way, Alex, and let's see if we can get them to move on," Jar said.

"Do you want me to hit them?" Alex's eyes were locked on the men in the distance. He was serious when he asked the question.

Jar smiled. "No, but get close enough to make them want to move."

I didn't know whether the rifle we had would shoot that far or not but I had heard that the range of a .22 was as much as a mile. If its range was only half that, Alex could splash some shots around them, though I doubted he could control them well enough to hit them.

He took plenty of time to aim carefully and squeezed off three shots. We couldn't tell at that distance where the shots fell, but they must have come near because the canoe started moving south off the canal to the right onto a tour boat and canoe trail that I knew went by Chesser Island and through Grand Prairie toward Blackjack Island. The trail was wide and fairly deep when rainfall was plentiful and was popular with day-trippers, but it was not a way out of the swamp.

Alex started replacing the three rounds and glanced once at Jar for instructions.

"Dad-*gummit*," Jar said with frustration. The direction Spanner and Markel were headed would just prolong their capture. It was after four o'clock and there was plenty of daylight left, but if they kept jerking us around they could make a desperate attempt in the dark to break the barriers set up and a lot of people could get hurt.

"Let's tell the Rangers what these guys are doing and get them to chase them down, Jar," I suggested. "Then, let's go home." The others gave nodded agreement.

Jar picked up the radio and started to speak when we heard the roar of a plane coming in fast.

Chapter 22

The white Cessna with green stripes came across Mizell Prairie from the east and skimmed in low over a small patch of cypress and pines on that side of the canal. It was the one with floats that Alex had seen on St. Mary's River. It crossed the canal about halfway between us and the turn-off to Grand Prairie where Spanner and Markel were and I could easily see the passenger in the open doorway that was rigged for drug drops like the other plane with wheeled landing gear. The passenger's right hand lifted to point toward us, and the craft suddenly banked sharply to the right, starting a circle around us. That maneuver gave him a perfect view of us and his hand dropped to his lap and came back up holding something black. It had to be a weapon and, judging from its bulk, it looked like another automatic.

"He's going to shoot!" Jar screamed. "Get down low!"

Chase was snapping pictures and finally stopped when I yelled his name. He stuffed his camera in an open pack and grabbed the gunwales to await the onslaught. The rest of us sat petrified and helpless too.

The fire pattern of bullets on the water started only a hundred yards from us on our right and snaked dizzily at first as if the shooter was determining where he was shooting; then the disturbance on the black surface seemed to spin off our way in almost a straight line. The impact on the water made a chunking sound and resonated through the murky liquid until we felt it drum in the canoes as it came nearer. The sharp repeated knocking of the gun above was heard too—even over the prolonged rumbling of the plane's engine. I glanced at the others and noticed Alex swinging the rifle toward the plane and took one last look at the watery path of bullets before ducking in reflex with my hands crossed behind my head. They were headed straight toward Chase.

In spite of all the racket from the plane, I still flinched when I heard the crack of Alex's rifle. It seemed to speak with an authority all its own and I noticed that the noise from the automatic weapon stopped suddenly. The second rifle shot sounded even louder without the competition and the air shuddered with the noise. I unfolded from my quailed position and swung to the right to pick up sight of the plane again just in time to see the weapon make a tumbling fall from the open door into shallow water behind us at the edge of the canal. A small puff of steam rose from the splash as the hot barrel cooled instantly from the bath.

The aircraft continued a tight circle around us and disappeared behind the group of trees to our left. It reappeared at almost the same place over the canal that it first came into view, but instead of continuing the circle, it headed toward Spanner and Markel. Alex pumped three more shots into the rear of the plane before running out of ammo. It was not without results because a good-size piece of rudder blasted off, exposing its inner framework, and a tear in the tail fin fluttered madly from the slice of a bullet as the rush of air pulled at the thin flap of metal until it reached a seam and it, too, ripped off.

The fast departure of the plane and the end of the shooting allowed me to partially gather my senses and I took inventory of the figures in front of me and noticed Chase missing from the canoe behind Jar and Alex.

"Chase!" I yelled. I jumped into the canal and half-walked on the peat mush and half-dog paddled toward the canoe that was in the line of fire a few moments ago. It had drifted a little sideways and I had to make my way around the stern, all the time expecting the worst. "Chase!"

"What?" I heard behind me. The tone was testy.

I spun around to Chase's sun-baked face and wet hair above the water surface. "Jesus, man," I retorted. "I thought you got hit. How did you get over there?" He was coming from behind the last in our string of canoes—a good fifty feet from the last place I saw him.

"How the fuck do I know? I flew over here with my Tinker Bell wings! Did you see that? That son-of-a-bitch almost shot me! Then he throws his fucking gun at me and I am pissed as hell!" He blew out a spray of peat-laced water that had made its way in during the tirade.

"'Throw,' hell," Byron said. "Alex shot that mother out of his hands. "Saw it after I ducked down and kissed my ass good-by. Couldn't help but look up and saw you swan dive off the canoe away from the bullets, Chase. You skittered across the water like a freaking water bug. Hooo-Weee! Alex, that was some kind of shooting! You opened up a can of 'Whup-Ass' on those guys!"

Chase made his way to the closest canoe, the middle one that I had occupied, grasped the gunwale and did a half-leapfrog across it and twisted so his feet and center of gravity landed in the gear in the middle of the floor, barely causing a ripple in the water. He leaned over the far side to compensate for most of my weight and I clawed my way in, with a last second lurch that almost sent us both over again.

"Jeez, Noble," Mr. Grace complained.

"Bite my ass," I hissed. I was only trying to save his by jumping in after him. Some gratitude.

We settled ourselves onto the seats and took up the watch with the others as the plane banked away from the canal and started its descent to the boat trail that led to Grand Prairie. I figured a thousand feet to land and maybe more to take off because of water resistance and they had well over that. The wet winter and recent rains provided water depth to keep all of the canoe trails open so far and the foot or so required for the landing floats would be no problem. The only obstructions they would encounter in the open expanse would be water lilies and their split round pads. We looked on helplessly while Jar radioed Bill Becker at the refuge compound.

"Beck, looks like they'll get out with the drugs. A white float plane with a green stripe is landing now near Chesser Island and as soon as they hook up with the two men in the canoe, they're gone. There's not enough time to get air boats there. Can the Fish and Wildlife 'copter give chase?"

"Not supposed to, Jar. Couldn't overtake and force them down anyway without the right firepower. The FBI's 'copter had mounted guns but it's in the water. We could try to keep track of them from a distance, but if they turn on us, we'll have to run. What about the Coast Guard?"

"They're our best bet, then. They want the drugs stopped too. I don't know if they'll come inland to intercept them, but I have a feeling this plane will head for the coast at a low altitude and turn south. Alex tore some skin off it with the rifle so they may have some rudder trouble."

"I'll call Colonel Heyward from here and let you know what he says," Becker said. "Are you coming in?"

"As soon as we grab a gun that fell from the plane and get these five horsepower egg beaters headed that way."

* * * *

We beached the canoes on the sandy soil alongside the concrete loading ramp. Clement and Dan, Jar's deputies, helped tie them off and started pulling camping gear out and placing it on the boat ramp. Several of the refuge staff stood by with radios near their boats or trucks awaiting instructions.

Everyone was aware of the progression of events in the swamp and the mood all around was in the low, dull range. Time and life can turn you up or down, from rage to skepticism to indifference, constantly changing from one to another to encourage alertness, unless you bottom out with a lack of feeling or fly high with an intensified sense of well being. Is peace and pleasure and success within that range or are they on a different scale? Maybe the ups and downs, yeas and nays, had just made us numb and left us without a trace of rank, power or character.

So very low.

Wearing their familiar smiles, Uncle Bob and Aunt Julia came out the door to the concession area and across the covered walk toward us. They, too, had to be aware of our troubles from conversations with others, overheard gossip, and reports blared on Chase's police scanner, but they forced a cheerful look anyway. By the time they got to the ramp they looked visibly shaken and I glanced around at ourselves and the canoes and saw why.

Hamp's arm was in a sling and blood had soaked through his bandage to the fresh tee shirt he put on at the barge. Alex's eye was a brownish-yellow and his split lip was still visible but not badly swollen. His and my arms and legs were cut, scratched and bug-bit the worst from trips through the jungle, and Chase and Byron came in a close second. Jar's thick curly red pelt on his arms and legs saved him from a lot of damage but his cheek and right ear had a bad scratch. Our clothes and bodies were torn, bloody and dirty and two-day beard growth and mussed hair definitely put us in the shipwreck survivor category. The faces I saw looked tired, hardened and cynical and I'm sure mine looked the same. Even Hamp's normally erect posture and square shoulders looked unusually burdened.

The canoes didn't look any better. The outsides were dirty and scratched by inhospitable swamp brush and brambles. Leaves and broken dry limbs littered the inside on unpacked wet tents and haphazard gear. The canoe Chase had spring-boarded from during the attack had taken on water and listed unhappily from nearly being overturned.

"Ty got here before the rain," Chase's dad explained to me. "I told him where the key was hidden at Hank and Dot's, so he should be there and rested up by now." Uncle Bob didn't quiz us about why he came back early, so I assumed Ty either told him or he filled in the blanks after assessing his shitty attitude.

I bit my lip from the thoughts of Ty messing up Mom's no doubt spotless kitchen like he did at the shelter, and if he chose my old room and bath to rest and clean up in, I might have to settle up with him if I didn't calm down some.

Mom and Dad always left for the North Georgia Mountains the morning of the day we were supposed to get back from our swamp trips. They normally stayed five or six days at a favorite cabin in Black Rock Mountain State Park and recuperated from preparations for the family reunion and rested up for the upcoming busy summer camping season at Stone's Throw. Hamp and I took care of the place during that time as a sort of working vacation, though the duties were minimal, and fed off the many leftovers from the past Sunday's get-together. We would return to Athens the following Sunday.

We didn't tell Chase's folks the mess Alex was in, having to turn in his dad and brother for transporting drugs and being forced to move out of his home. All that could come later since our appearance was shock enough for the time being, so we concentrated on loading coolers and personal gear onto "Green", Dad's old Easter egg-colored truck, and Alex's truck. We were separating Alex's things from ours so he could go straight home, and it surprised me when he said he was going to Stone's Throw.

"Before I go to the authorities, I'm going to get my stuff out of the house," he said. "If they seize the house and belongings because of this drug thing, I'd be left without anything. It'll be dark in a little while, so I'll just camp out on the pavilion and go in the morning. I don't want to sleep at home tonight—in fact, I don't want to be alone tonight or tomorrow. I guess I need family with me."

Alex was seldom that outspoken. If he wasn't working or caring for Grady, he went along with the crowd in whatever was planned on our outings and quietly participated. On occasion, we would get a reaction from him in the form of good-humored complaint when he was at the bottom of our human "Stone Pile"—a situation resulting from inappropriate behavior by one of the group such as hotdogging, petty goading, deep thinking, or even dressing strangely. STONE PILE! is loudly announced by someone, and subsequent piling on by the offended renders the offender helpless, if not bruised or shaken, between the ground and several hundred pounds of humanity like a football pileup. The guys on my construction jobs in Athens called this custom a "Dog Pile" but around Folkston there were usually enough Stones involved to call it otherwise. We usually did it to Alex to break down his defenses and get him to loosen up a little. Our adventures were incomplete unless we got a smile, laugh or some sort of rise out of him. A fellow needs to have some fun—throw away the bookmark and lose his place every once in a while.

"I'll camp with you," I said. "And I'll help get your things tomorrow in old Green." I took one of the wet tents from the rental gear pile to use that night for protection against mosquitoes. It would dry easily before bedtime.

Hamp grabbed another tent and Chase got the third. "Count me in too," Byron said. "We haven't officially camped out yet and we have one more night on our outing. I want to try some of that South African wine Hamp's been bragging about—I might even try some of that Mexican beer if it doesn't have a worm in it."

"It's the kind without it," Jar said patiently. "I'll join you guys when I can pull away. I ought to stay here and brief Beck and be sure county people are not needed any more before I go, but I'll get there when I can. I need to sleep in my car near the radio and phone, though, just in case. We can all help Alex move first thing in the morning and then he and I can get with the Ware County Sheriff and the DEA about Grady and Tucker. I think Gus Bunner's hands are going to be full trying to get that Black Hawk helicopter out of the bog."

Alex seemed to breathe a sigh of relief. No need him going through all that alone when he's got family and friends. Besides, our appetite for the wild had not been properly sated—not without being around a big campfire in our underwear, occasionally breaking into doleful howls or penetrating screams, grunting spontaneously, and emitting other bodily noises fueled by baked potatoes and foamy beer. There would also have to be inspired tall tales, my specialty, and carefully thought-out pranks, Chase's forte. Reentry into civilization would be difficult unless we decompressed with basic human behavior that has been displayed from generation to generation by our ancestors.

* * * *

Before we left, Becker joined us to update us on the Coast Guard search for the float plane. After it picked up Spanner and Markel with the drugs, it headed due east like Jar thought it would. Then the Forestry Service tracked it from a distance until two Coast Guard 'copters scrambled from their station on the coast. Forestry gave them the location and heading of the drug plane and returned to base for budget reasons. Their small craft was falling well behind the fast Cessna anyway. That was the last anyone saw of the float plane and a comprehensive ground and air search was underway. Disappearing into thin air was apparently possible in our little world.

We piddled with the gear as if nothing unusual was happening and Becker was simply telling us the outcome of the Braves' opener. Disappointment and shock no longer fazed us…not until we finished emptying the canoe Chase had jumped from and saw the holes in a pack and cooler. Then we saw three bullet holes in the hull where he lounged just before the air attack.

We had to stop to gather our senses and let our trembling subside. For some reason, tears welled in my eyes at the sight. Jar stared in disbelief at the holes that could have been through Chase too. Hamp and Byron walked off in different directions a short distance, Hamp slowly shaking his lowered head and Byron staring at the sky with his thumbs hooked on his back pockets. Chase just sat on the ground with his arms resting on shaky knees, his head faced downward in thoughts of the gravity of the scene. We almost came back one short that trip.

No one could have kept us apart that night.

Chapter 23

I heard the front screen door slam even though the house was a hundred yards from the fire pit where we were setting up camp. That was always a sore spot for Mom, or so she made out, because she thought kids had the time to slow down enough to close the spring-loaded door quietly while in a hurry and loaded down with cookies or cold biscuits or the current set of toys and unauthorized household items needed for the next few hours of play. "Don't slam the screen door!" she would always yell before or after it was slammed but we never got punished for the infraction. The simple fact of the matter was that screen doors slammed all over the country at any given moment and it was these sounds of people going to and fro that confirmed life on the planet. It was like a heartbeat or the click of a valve or the pound of a foot to let us know that the human race was up and running. Deep down, I think Mom knew all that because I've caught her smiling more than once at the familiar sound even before her nest was empty. She just had to fuss about it because her mother did.

The door slam announced that Ty would be headed our way and when he got nearer, his thin body barely made a shadow across the yard, but the one it made was fifty feet long in the late afternoon sun. He passed the pavilion and made his way toward our camping area. He and Alex were about the same height and weight, but Alex was more sinewy and healthy looking, especially after the sun and exercise he got the last two days. Unlike Alex and his brother, Ty looked soft and weak and his heavily gelled and perfectly combed dark hair looked out of place south of Macon. He wore dark blue polyester pants and a white short-sleeve shirt with a button-down collar and had on brown tassel loafers and white socks. All he needed was his clip-on tie and he would be ready to sell used cars in Tennessee.

Scratch and Sniff preceded him, making restless happy shadows of their own as they bounded down the worn path. They were Mom and Dad's ageless yard dogs, each from uncommon ancestors but both smart and faithful to a fault. Scratch fell behind to scratch an itch that couldn't wait. He had a skin condition that flared up sometimes and was compared to a human's seborrhea that no amount of salves, ointments or pills could abate. His snout pointed upward and his eyes closed as he dug into his side with his claws and his lips curled into a satisfied smile.

Sniff got to us first and she proceeded to make the rounds smelling our crotches for identification purposes, the momentum of her wagging tail getting her hind legs out of step. She spent extra time on Byron's junction to make sure he was qualified with the Stone smell to be there. Byron finally had to shoo her away, admitting he could smell himself too and promising to shower as soon as camp was set up. She turned her attention to the odors of each piece of camping gear as if she could tell where we had been and what we had done. Scratch finally caught up and collected a pat on the head from each of us. Feeling satisfied, he fell asleep near the fire pit to wait on supper while Sniff chased the fat ducks that were inching our way for a handout back to the pond where they were supposed to be.

"I was starting to worry about you guys," Ty said. "Did you run into any problems?"

"We had a few," I said. "The guys on the island got away with the drugs."

"Gosh, I'm surprised, considering all the people trying to get them. Y'all aren't going to sleep in the house?" So much for his interest in our day. *Be cool, Noble.*

"Naw, thought we would try to camp out one night without interruption even if it's not in the swamp. The moon's still full, so we can enjoy that."

"Well, I've had my fill of it. I couldn't stay another night out, moon or not. Say, *Forrest Gump* is on TV again tonight. Why don't y'all come up and watch it. I've seen it three times."

"Not me," I said.

I turned the movie off soon after Tom Hanks started running and didn't even rewind the rental. I'd rather watch paid programming. At least those people had a job and earned what they got. I never liked Hanks in a movie after that even though he was just acting the part.

"I'll pass," Chase said as he piled charcoal high on a grill.

"Me too," Byron joined in.

Hamp's reply was not aloud. *Hump Gump.*

"Oh, by the way, Noble," Ty said. "A wrecker is supposed to haul off the Chrysler tomorrow. Everything is taken care of by the insurance company."

I started to ask him if he included Dad's wheelbarrow in the loss but thought better of it. Assembly probably wouldn't be covered anyway.

"Also," Ty added, "I bought bus tickets to Memphis leaving tomorrow morning at ten, Byron, so don't stay up and drink too much so you can be packed and ready to go early. We need to be in town by 9:30 to pick them up."

"I'm not going," Byron said.

* * * *

Talk about freeze-framing a scene. To a person, all action stopped. We were just finishing setting up camp on the pavilion side of the fire pit so the wind would carry the smoke out across the little fishing pond and not across us. We were the only tent campers at Stone's Throw that early in the week so we bent the rules a little on placement of tents and scattering of gear. The weekends during the spring were the only time private tent areas were assigned anyway because the busy weekday season really didn't start until after school let out for the summer. Some campers liked to mingle anyway, so if any of the motor campers hooked up in the back spaces wanted to sit by our fire and watch us cut up, they could join us. Everyone was welcome at our family get-togethers at Stone's Throw including total strangers. If it were otherwise, Mom and Dad were in the wrong business.

I had my shaving kit and towel ready to head to the public showers and take a much-needed bath but I stayed around out of courtesy when Ty came down. I was glad I did because I was the most talkative of the four campers. My heart really wasn't in it but I felt like I kept our silence from being rude. When Byron told Ty he wasn't going back with him, I gladly turned the floor over to him and tried to look natural so I could take in the rest of the conversation.

"What do you mean, 'You're not going?'" Ty predictably started out. A vein in his smooth white temple stood out a little like county road 138 with the dogleg on the north end near the sand pumps.

"Just what I said, Ty. There's nothing for me in Memphis. I need to get away from that place."

"Of course there's something there—your family, your work. It's a big city and it has so much more to offer than down here."

"Sure, there's you and Mom and Dad, and I love y'all. And there's the work. But you know what? Y'all don't need me—any day laborer picked up on any corner could do what I do. I can't sell cars and I'm not good with all those fancy figures y'all use and I just don't need to be there. For me, it's a nowhere job and I want out. As far as whether I'll stay here, I don't know. I have a lot of thinking to do. I do know that Memphis is not in the running, though."

Go for it, Byron.

"Byron, you're not thinking straight. We have a family business and the profits are shared. Our needs are met and then some. If you strike out on your own you'll get a rude awakening. You had it made in Memphis and you are throwing it all away. Don't you want security?"

"Don't you see? Security is nothing if I can't live with myself. I know y'all mean well, but when have I made a decision for myself? You and Dad have determined my options and made my decisions for me. You've directed me around like I was a little kid, and come payday I get my allowance. You are trying to protect me from the world and I've ended up just a toy with a heartbeat that doesn't get to come out of the toy box.

"I can be somebody down here. I can think on my own. I might even be trusted to carry a gun and use a radio. I could help capture two drug runners and somebody might risk his life and get shot to keep me from being shot. You wouldn't understand any of that because your perfect world is up in Tennessee and you only come here to rest up from it once in a while. I see a future down here or some place like this where people don't treat me like a dummy. I want to be challenged and earn what I get. I also want to feel at home and alive and in the last three days I've felt more that way than whatever existence I ever had in Memphis. There, the two of us didn't even make a whole. With me gone there'll be two of us.

"This is not just a practice run or a trial offer that will expire—it's a flight from and a flight to. It's and emergency. If I mess up, I'll keep looking ahead, but not toward Memphis. I'll still love you and Mom and Dad, and by doing this, I think y'all will love me more. At least respect for me will be a part of that love."

Ty didn't say anything for a while. He wasn't scornful, nor did he turn on his heel in a huff. He just looked at Byron like he had never seen him before and I thought some of that respect was already budding. I wished Dad could have heard Byron—I know his words changed me and my respect for him.

"OK," Ty finally said. "We'll stay in touch and I'll get your things to you."

"That would be great."

Chapter 24

By the time we shaved, showered and checked each other's backs for ticks, the giant mound of coals on the grill was consumed in a hot glow and ready for the thick rib eyes. Foil-wrapped baking potatoes were already in place and would be ready when the meat quit moving and we finished our first beer. We had run out of hot water about halfway through the showers but it didn't seem to quench our need to get clean. It was probably just as well because the cold well water helped to numb the chigger bites and our libidos. Many of my bites were on my 'nad bag and a couple of the mighty mites roamed to the end of my unit and dug in. Modesty wouldn't allow too much scratching while naked in view of others because I might not be able to stop, but I thought of a great way of relieving the itch if Bonnie had come down. I'd just have to make do later by myself.

We ate pretty much in silence other than a grunt or two, partly from our hunger for meat thicker than a dime and partly from discomfort over Byron's verbal encounter with Ty when he announced he was not going back to Memphis. No telling how long Byron had wanted to make the break from control by his family but the gnawing was finally over and he had expressed himself well. I had an idea Ty would be the toughest of his family to convince because you seldom saw them apart, so the hardest part was over. I was glad there were apparently no hard feelings on either side when their cases were made, but the exchange was intense to witness and I for one hesitated to start a conversation that might eventually lean back that way.

The tense mood was finally swung the other way after a few beers and swigs from the wine bottles and it was done by the two among us who were struggling the most.

Scratch and Sniff had wolfed down our scraps and settled down near the fire in front of us with an eye out in case something else cropped up. Soon Sniff held her nose to the air and picked up a smell that had to be checked out and she disappeared through the empty campground and into the woods beyond on a quest. In less than an hour, she would be headed back the other way on the trail of something unseen by us but equally as important. Scratch saw no need to waste such energy but he had a sudden discomfort from gnats, fleas or his skin condition and he jerked up to a sitting position and hiked up one leg for easy access to the offended area and commenced to nibbling and licking himself. For a while it seemed natural for Scratch—even the accompanying grunts and groans—but I was beginning to wonder after a good five minutes. We all maintained our straight faces but it was getting harder and harder.

Finally, Byron said, "Damn, if I could do that, I never would leave the house."

Before the laughter erupted, Alex squeezed in, "Wouldn't have to range far, that's for sure."

* * * *

With the tension broken, the rest of the evening and up until around two o'clock in the morning was a great time. Jar rolled in around eleven with very little news coming from the swamp. Gus Bunner had arranged for a Skycrane chopper to remove the disabled Blackhawk at night before the press got wind of it and interfered with his efforts the next day, whatever they were to be. The Coast Guard called off their air search of the white Cessna at dark and had plans to resume at daybreak. They continued to comb ocean inlets and coves within twenty miles of St. Marys with every available boat. Other stations along the coast were put on watch alert. Ground forces of the Guard, law officers of nearby counties and other available agencies checked possible hiding places on the ground, since the float plane had wheeled landing gear too.

Jar took a quick shower and decided against a shave since his beard was so light colored. We gave him his very own bottle of wine to save passing-around time and he almost caught up with us. We all called it quits with a good buzz on when the fire died down and we were too lazy to gather more wood. Before I fell asleep, I remember a slight breeze that lightly rang two of the three sides of the harbor wind bell I gave Mom for Christmas and a swirl of sparks danced obediently toward the pond before they, too, switched off for the night.

* * * *

We were up and had breakfast going by seven Wednesday morning. The slight headache I had was well worth it and after a big breakfast of bacon and scrambled eggs and two cups of Hamp's Jamaican Blue Mountain coffee, I was good to go. We had a big day ahead, or at least an unsettling one, so we just lowered our heads and got with it. Jar and Byron finished first and took Ty into town to collect his ticket and wait on the bus. Mcdonald's wasn't far from the station so he could spend the time there and have breakfast with the city folks. I bet we had the best coffee, though. By the time they returned, we had the trucks emptied and the tents struck and the gear was neatly stacked on a picnic table in the pavilion. It would be OK there while we picked up Alex's things. Byron rode with Jar in the cruiser and Alex drove his truck and I took Green. Hamp brought up the rear in his Land Rover.

Alex lived about halfway between St. Marys and Folkston near a community called Kingsland. The Slappey home wasn't grand by any means when compared to the fine old southern plantation homes spared by Sherman on his way to Fort McCallister and so lovingly cared for by generations of old money. It did have a long straight driveway flanked by mossy live oaks and an occasional regal magnolia and it did make a big loop in front of a single, though not double, set of steps leading up nearly seven feet to the main level—the only living level.

The ground level contained the stone pillars and creosoted wood piers that were foundation for the house to keep it above floodwaters from the St. Marys River the one time, so far, it reached the house in 1918. An old barrel stave was fitted around a stone pier and secured at the high water mark by my grandfather and he scratched his initials and the date deep in the mortar. The marker was only eighteen inches above the ground but served as a reminder of what could happen to houses built too low in the low country.

The foundation was shielded from view by white latticework that was falling to disrepair since Grady's accident and death of Alex's stepmother. Alex had little time for maintenance on the house with his two jobs but off the end of the long front porch he did make time to build a handicap ramp that sloped gently down to a wide landing and from there sloped the rest of the way to the ground in the opposite direction. The ramp allowed Grady to get out of the house in his electric wheelchair on his own and motor down the winding flat paved walkway the two hundred yards to a mossy, dank screened cabana and boat dock on the river. Except for the path and a mowed width of grass on each side, the yard to the river was thick with a growth of palmetto, Loblolly bay and small pines and privet shrubs.

The house itself was single story but the huge rooms had tall ceilings, and with a high-pitched roof and on the tall foundation, it had an imposing look. Instead of reaching a single ridge at the peak, the hip-style metal roof stopped short and there was a flat area of roof about eight feet square that may have once been a widow's walk but the rail around it, if there ever was one, was long gone. A waterproof trap door led to the high vista from a sturdy ladder in the attic.

Deep porches with roofs of less pitch than the main house had simple white balustrades and ran along the front, back and one side, and part of the side porch was screened for a sleeping porch. Tall windows and doors had real hinged and latch-able shutters. With its lap siding, the overall look of the house might be called coastal or tidewater design.

I always enjoyed visiting there even though Alex was five years younger than me. When we were older, I would drop around sometimes with friends. The big back yard was mostly open back then and invited any type ball game, and the wide lazy river was a constant source of entertainment. After I started going to UGA, I would visit during holidays but I chose to stay in Athens after graduation and the visits weren't as frequent. Two years later, Alex lost his mom to cancer and two years after that, his stepmother died and Grady was crippled. Things were never the same with Grady. He would stay mostly to himself but I still never felt welcome there. Alex was always uncomfortable too. Whenever Hamp and I went back, we always picked Alex up and went other places for fun, if we could get Alex to have any. Thus estranged from the place, I still hated to see it go to someone without Stone blood. I'm sure that was part of Alex's hurt and bitterness, too.

* * * *

We pulled off the crushed stone loop to the side of the house with the sleeping porch. There was another set of steps there and it was the most direct way to Alex's bedroom. We were out of the vehicles and stretching from the twenty-minute trip when we heard the crunch of tires on the drive. Three black GMC Suburbans with heavily tinted windows came down the drive in perfect formation, stopped together, and the front and back doors on all three cars came open as if the same detonator set off charges in each one. All but three men labeled DEA had on the familiar dark blue tee shirts with yellow FBI on the back. Gus Bunner had on a blue windbreaker to distinguish himself and make himself sweat in the morning heat. He stepped forward with his hand up as if to halt a galloping posse in an old western. The posse remained at the cars.

"Well, well, well," he said as he strolled up in his high-water pants. "Look who's here. Fancy meeting you here."

Jeez. He was a walking cliché. I started to say, "Look what the cat drug in," but thought better of it.

Alex was closest and Bunner stepped up to him and held his head up as if looking through bifocals, only he didn't have on glasses, and said, "Who are you?"

Bad choice of us to pick on if anyone had asked me.

In evenly measured words, Alex stared him in the eye and asked, "Who-the-fuck-are-you?"

Bunner was visibly shaken but recovered quickly. "Just a minute, young man. You just as well drop the attitude. I'm Special Agent Gus Bunner with the FBI and this is not a social call." He flipped his ID open and closed in a quick sleight of hand movement like he was pressed for time. "Now give me a name."

"My name, Special Agent Gus Bunner, is Mr. Alex Stone Slage and this is my home—or was until about three o'clock yesterday afternoon. I'm here to get my things, most of which I have receipts for, and I understand that I have two weeks to get my possessions out. If you know different, let me know. Otherwise, I'm headed up these steps to my room."

"You're Grady Slage's boy?"

"I was until I started getting hair between my legs." A couple of the agents that were paying attention gave a little chuckle. The rest of us near Alex just stood by quietly with a newfound respect for him. He, like Byron, needed the freedom he had gained by cutting ties and he was already displaying the confidence that went with it.

"Where's your dad?" Bunner asked gruffly.

"In Miami, I guess. Looking for a place to live, same as I'll be doing, but not there."

"Miami! What the hell's he doing there? That wasn't in the plan! Does he have a death wish?"

"Hold on just a minute, Bunner," Jar said. "Sounds like you have put one of us at risk and I'm not liking it. I want to know what's going on and I want to know *now*."

"Jarrett, you stay out of this. We're not even in your county. I told you before, this is a routine FBI matter and we'll call you if you are needed when you get off vacation."

"Routine? Was it routine to refuse help and let two smugglers slip through your hands with two million in drugs and to cost the taxpayers another million to fix a helicopter?"

I could tell that Bunner was surprised and embarrassed that Jar knew about the swamp incident. Apparently no one had told him that we were on the island while the fiasco was going on. Or maybe it just wasn't important enough for him to hear it.

Jar's red face was clashing with his copper hair but his voice remained calm. "If I'm reading between the lines right, you are using a wheelchair-bound citizen as bait in one of your crazy plans and his life is in danger. Am I close?"

Alex was trembling and I squeezed his shoulder a couple of times in an effort to calm him. If he joined in at that moment, it might be physically.

Bunner grimaced as he looked toward each of us. There was no eye contact and his fingers rubbed nervously against his thumbs as if he was checking the feel of a fabric. He began speaking reluctantly.

"About six weeks ago Grady Slage called my office with information about a suspicious plane flying low over the swamp. It rang true enough with data that we and the DEA already had but wasn't enough to go on at the time, so I asked him to ask around and keep an eye out for more flights and any patterns he might notice. He had also become suspicious of his stepson, Tucker Langston, because of his questions about personnel activity at the swamp that he might get from Alex and because of Tucker's involvement with a suspect security company that we already had a file on. It didn't take long to justify opening an official investigation when we started checking on owners and employees of several companies that had connections."

"Safepoint, Transpoint and Southpoint," Jar said.

The agent looked at Jar quizzically, but continued. "We checked every activity and lead that Slage informed us of and pretty soon most of you were under our surveillance and also that of our suspects. We were needing fresh information fast. We had picked up on Monday as the regular drop day and wanted to move quickly because we learned from the Coast Guard that the drug drop operation was flexible and subject to change at any time. We decided to make our move when we heard that the two men were on the island. We already had men and equipment nearby."

"If Dad was working with you all along," Alex said, "Why weren't we let in on what was going on? You knew we weren't in on the drug deals."

"The more people that knew them would make it easier for our plans to go bust. We had to be as secretive and alert as the drug runners were and it couldn't be done with a lot of people in on it. It was no reflection against anyone—especially you. He was following my wishes."

"Why would Grady be in danger in Miami?" Jar asked. "Because he was going to be with Tucker?"

"If he went down there to stir up trouble with Tucker Slage's associates, he could be in danger. He wouldn't know who they were, though, because nobody's told him. Look, before you ask any more questions, let me explain something—this place is not sold and you are moving out for nothing and there's no reason for Grady Slage to be in Miami."

Chapter 25

We stood in the shade of the tall old house in a semicircle facing Bunner. A light humid breeze came up from the river with its river smells and played with the more delicate vegetation around the perimeter of the yard before tiring and coming to rest. A flock of noisy crows complained nearby, probably to a trespassing hawk, and temporarily drowned out the mid-morning buzz of insects. Bunner's voice was the only human sound, his men smoking or dozing in the long black cars with all their doors still open.

His statement got no verbal reaction from us because it would have served no purpose other than to delay the explanation. After all, part of our solution to the puzzle was shot to hell anyway since Cousin Grady wasn't in with the bad guys, so we had little to contribute. I had a kind of helpless feeling like being up against unknown forces in the deepest dark with no control over either. There was no need to take even a wild guess as to what was going on or to try and ask an intelligent question, so we listened quietly to Bunner.

"While our investigation was gaining momentum, Tucker approached Grady for money to start a courier business in Miami. He painted a pretty picture for his step-dad that he could get better medical help down there and that he would realize a quick return on his investment. He said he knew of someone that was interested in buying him out and they could be down there in a month. Grady saw through all that from the start because he had helped him before and got little in return but promises, so the request was refused. He also knew from other information we shared with him that the place would be an ideal transfer point for drugs due to its remote location on a big river with access to the ocean. When I learned about the opportunity to sell in one of our phone conversations, we decided to meet and discuss it some more. At the time, I was still unsure of what we were dealing with and how far-reaching it was. I had already found out that the more we learned about the operation, the bigger it got.

"At the meeting we hatched a plan to make Tucker think Grady would sell the place and help him after all. In doing so, it would help smoke out other people Tucker was connected with, or at least give us a clearer trail toward those that were working behind corporate names. We got what we hoped for and more from names on the sales contract and the people Tucker started contacting in Miami when he thought he could get some help from Grady. There was no need for a fake closing because we had what we wanted. Grady strung Tucker along by giving a bogus date for the closing and telling him he was in contact with the closing attorney and the buyer's representative. Tucker was apparently busy coordinating Monday's drug drop so he never questioned the arrangements. Grady was supposed to disappear for a while after the non-existent closing so he wouldn't have to deal with Tucker when he discovered there was no closing and started to squirm. In the meantime we are linking as many people as possible to Tucker, the people on the sales contract, and the three 'point' companies and getting ready to pick them up."

"Do you have enough on anyone to pick them up on drug charges?" Jar asked. "All you have now is a couple of Hispanics on assault and weapons charges."

Bunner gave him a questioning look again but went ahead and answered. "Combined with information from some of our stalled cases, we can get some fairly high-ups connected to the drug operation. We are also still hoping to find the plane that flew out of the swamp with the drugs. We may end up in a plea bargaining situation with some but we also may get some informers and make some more serious charges. It's the risk we have to take. The more turmoil and pressure we keep them under, the harder it is for them to operate. Grady Slage definitely helped us tie some loose ends together with his cooperation."

"At the expense of his safety, looks like," Jar added coldly.

"The deal was to stay in one of our safe houses in Jacksonville for a few weeks. I haven't checked with them but he should be there. Don't worry, he's not as dumb as his step-son thinks he is—the wheelchair must make Tucker think the whole package is impaired."

Out of the corner of my eye, I noticed Alex staring at the ground and combing his fingers through his long hair. When he became aware I was watching, he looked up with a half-smile. He was feeling better about some things.

"You're Byron S. Slappey, aren't you?" Bunner asked, looking through the imaginary bifocals.

"That'd be me."

"You're the only one I don't have a picture and bio of. I'll have to ask that you come down to Jacksonville with the others to give statements concerning your knowledge of the drug operation and the apprehension of the two naked suspects." Bunner almost cracked a smile but if he had it might have cracked his face. "It'll be tomorrow before we can get that in motion if that's agreeable with you all. Deputy Manager Becker has provided me with a brief account of your involvement including the alerting of his people and county personnel. We're just getting out of the swamp and have several preliminary meetings back at the office before we'll have enough interviewers. I can send a car in the morning but there may be a wait for a car in the afternoon when we're done."

"We'll make do," Hamp said.

"Good. Let's make it nine o'clock." Bunner gave Alex a card. "By the way, Sheriff Jarrett, since you have been on vacation and have no first hand knowledge of what went on, you don't have to come unless you just want to."

Jar grinned. "I might ought to come along."

"I thought so."

Bunner advised us as he got in his Surburban that two of his men were hidden up on the highway in a dark sedan like Safepoint's and had the place under surveillance. He cautioned Hamp not to let the air out of the tires. With that, all the doors closed in unison and they headed up the shaded drive as one.

We stood in silence as we watched the last set of taillights turn right onto the road to Jacksonville.

Alex finally turned and said, "We need to start getting my stuff before it gets so hot."

Chapter 26

It's amazing the things you can accumulate in a lifetime. Not that I was that old, but I already had taken up Hamp's double garage with my construction tools and workshop, and the big pantry off the kitchen was my darkroom. I had some necessities in the living room like my recliner and stereo but we used Hamp's TV because it was a thirty-six incher. My twenty-seven was in my room placed so I, and sometimes Bonnie, could watch it from a queen-size bed with a top-of-the-line mattress set. The rest of the big bedroom was filled with non-matching pieces I traded work for with a guy that was a little short of cash. My computer took up a corner of the room where I kept track of my business records and checked E-mail offering programs for breast enhancement and a big choice of "adult toys, video, magazines, and more." I could even get an international driver's license if I wanted to. Other pieces of furniture in the house were probably mine but we had had them since our college-days apartment and ownership gets a little fuzzy after a while.

Clothing was another matter. If I put everything neatly folded or hung in its place the volume would seem far less than the way my room looked back home. My dirty pile was starting to encroach on the clean pile and the different type shoes I wear were in a handy ragged line about four feet from the bed so I wouldn't trip on them if I had to get up at night. We found Alex's room in a similar condition.

"Jeez, Alex," I said when we stepped in his room. I didn't feel as much the slob that Bonnie Gill made me out to be.

"Screw you, Noble. This won't take any time at all."

He took the light blanket that was wadded up at the foot of the bed and spread it out and started pitching clean clothes onto it, and occasionally throwing in a breakable, like a picture or bottle of cologne, to be cushioned in the bulk. The rest of us picked up on the program and soon had the corners of the blanket and two sheets tied together in giant balls of possessions. Pillow cases were handy to use in the same manner, and Alex found large heavy-duty garbage bags for shoes and dirty clothing.

Jar was able to squeeze the computer equipment and nineteen-inch TV in the extended cab area of Alex's truck and use towels and pillows to protect them from each other. Chase and Byron piled all the clothing on hangers on the back seat of Jar's cruiser and there was room for little else. His trunk was still full of his camping and crime fighting gear. There were almost enough boxes for all the books and they went in the back of the Range Rover. I took a tall stack of loose ones to wedge into the voids and noticed a Ken Follett book I hadn't read. I put it within easy reach with plans to ask Alex if I could borrow it.

I was jealous of Alex for having a nicer miter saw than I had. Mine was an old 8 ½ inch DeWalt Crosscutter which served me well but I couldn't help but lust for his twelve-inch compound job. Judging by the neat work he did on the handicap ramp, he must have bought it for that project. All the joints were "tight as goat lips" as my men and I would say of work that was acceptable or better. We eventually shortened it to "lips" and grew to revel in the sound of that word.

Tools and other items that wouldn't be harmed were put in Green's rusty bed, some protected in garbage bags. The rest of the belongings were squeezed in the Dodge's lined bed and the mattress and box spring was lashed on top with rope that Chase brought. We would have to park it under the pavilion when we got back to Stone's Throw in case of another afternoon rain.

"That about it?" Chase asked Alex while we drank Cokes on the front porch. The faint whine of a log or pulpwood cutter sounded off to the north, probably miles away.

"There's some fishing tackle and a cooler down at the river I want to get and we'll call it quits."

"You're sure...," Chase started the question that would have been better asked before everything was loaded. He squirmed a little, probably hoping he wasn't heard.

"I'm sure. It's for the best."

I was pretty sure we all felt that way. It just had to be said.

Byron wanted to get something out too. "Maybe the unhappiness just sneaked up by degrees and accumulated until there was no comfort to be found. Maybe Grady just needed independence—needed to be useful."

"And that wasn't possible with me in the way," Alex said. "I had both lanes of traffic stopped—mine and his."

I admired Alex for picking up on his dad's need for freedom when it was finally displayed and that his feelings weren't hurt that he was used to gain information and the purpose withheld from him. He saw the solution quickly and took action. Seems like when you admit a mistake, it opens up ways to correct it. I liked the newly transformed Alex. I still liked Ty too.

* * * *

"I'll help with the tackle," I said. "We'll be hungry by the time we get back to Stone's Throw so we should get going."

We stepped around the house and picked up the asphalt path to the cabana. Birds and other creatures barely seen skittered ahead of us into the shadows of vegetation that had taken over the yard years ago. Competition for sunlight was fierce, and some trees the size of my wrist were thirty feet tall to get their pitiful foliage high enough to suck in the light. Only the lazy curving path gave any hint of civilization that should be at either end and it, too, would succumb to the crushing roots and creeping vines if it weren't for regular maintenance.

The trail meandered roughly parallel to a slightly curving creek with tall, steep banks that made its way to the river where we were headed. In most places the edge of the bank was obscured by undergrowth except where access was maintained to allow fishing for Channel catfish in the food-churned water. The last two hundred feet of creek before the river became progressively wider and deeper from river backwater.

As we started rounding the last bend in the walkway before coming into view of the cabana and dock, Alex suddenly dropped to a squat and I instinctively did the same. It annoyed me that I had become so punchy and I said, "What the hell is it?"

Alex craned his neck and looked to the right toward the mouth of the creek and whispered, "There's the plane."

Chapter 27

We were at a point where the curving path was near the creek and the vegetation was thinned out for access to it and I saw the white of the familiar plane. It had been pulled backward into the mouth of the creek and it was in the deep shadows of the thick tree canopy overhead. The creek banks were deep and wide enough to obscure all but the tops of the wings and the tail section was pulled around and tipped up onto the bank. Three men were standing or stooping near it busily working on the sections damaged by Alex's marksmanship and I saw the heads of three others that were sitting nearby. The size of the missing pieces of the lightweight skin looked bigger up close so apparently it affected the plane's performance enough to have to land quickly and repair them. Luckily, the drug runners had the newly-acquired property, or so they thought, to hide on and make the repairs.

I craned my neck to see if there were any more people at the dock or cabana and saw no one, but I could see the back of a big white boat with tall twin Mercurys and the green logo of Safepoint Security on the side. It must have brought repairmen and parts for the plane.

"What should we do?" Alex asked.

"Go back to the house and get Jar to call the Coast Guard and have them come up the river by water and air. Have him call Camden County for backup and an ambulance. The FBI won't have time to get here, but he can alert the ones on surveillance up on the highway. Then, all y'all bring guns to this point but wait on my signal before moving up on them. You'll need to spread out and go in at different points through the brush to hem them up. You'll have to move fast so they won't have a chance to cross the creek and get in the woods."

"What about you?"

"First off, I'm going to turn that boat loose—we don't want them to have a way to leave. Then, when I start to hear the helicopter, I'll create a distraction."

God, I had started to hate that word.

✳ ✳ ✳ ✳

I watched Alex sprint out of sight toward the house and I ducked left into the thick growth and carefully made a semi-circle around to the far side of the cabana from where the plane was. When I got into the clearing I stayed low in case someone was sitting in the building. The lower forty inches of its walls was siding, like the house, and the entire upper part was screened. As I crept along the side I thought I detected murmurs and heavy breathing but I didn't dare look in.

The riverbank started to slope off toward the water about halfway along the side of the cabana and created a dark muddy crawl space under its floor. Thick pilings held up that end and also served to anchor the dock, which was parallel to the structure. Metal rings on the dock encircled the two end pilings and allowed the level of the floating dock to fluctuate with that of the river. I would have to crawl under the building to untie the boat because the screened wall on the side of the river went all the way to the floor and there was a chance I would be seen.

I started under the old building and the musty smells of old creosote and moldy wood tried to take my breath but the heavy damp air invaded my lungs anyway. I heard restless movement above, so I would have to take it slow and easy. The skim of mud on the bank pulled off the sandy soil and stuck to my boat shoes and hands and increased with each step until its weight pulled it off to start over again. Several slips caused my right hip to land on the dark brown mud but it helped with traction to keep from slipping under the dock barrels.

Frogs the size of chickens jumped in the water ahead of my intrusion and I was sure any moment that someone would appear on the far side where the screen door was to check on the splashes. I learned to move slowly because I started out fast in a monkey-walk and drug my backbone under the sharp corner of a joist and skinned about four vertebrae in a row.

I reached the mooring for the bow and stretched across the narrow dock on my stomach to the cleat and undid the rope. Returning to the shadows of the building and pilings, I scooted to the stern rope and did the same. The twenty-foot boat started easing away from the dock in the lazy current and I gave it a gentle nudge to speed up the process. When it got farther out, the current would be faster and take it out of swimming range if it was spotted.

I backtracked to the other end and crawled to the front corner. Slowly stretching up near the corner, I looked over the ledge right into the face of Charlene Luther.

I almost cried out—partly from the shock of seeing someone and partly because she looked so bad. Her hair was a tangled mess and her makeup was either smudged or gone. She squirmed on her bed of boat cushions and whimpered feverishly. Old dark blood covered a makeshift bandage on her right arm, which rested heavily on the floor. She needed to see a doctor fast.

* * * *

When I started hearing the Coast Guard, I wasn't sure Jar had had the time to get everyone lined up and to get in place at the bend in the walk. The helicopter must have been continuing yesterday's search for the plane and was nearby. I hadn't even thought up a distraction. All I could come up with was to yell at the top of my lungs and hope it drew the attention of the ones at the plane so our side could spread out and move in.

"HOLD IT RIGHT THERE!...DON'T ANYBODY MOVE!... YOU'RE ALL UNDER ARREST!"

Jeez. That was as hackneyed as one of Gus Bunner's conversations.

"REACH FOR THE FUCKING SKY!" Hell, you could run out of those things after a while—especially under pressure. I would catch plenty of crap about that one later.

I heard the yelling and confusion taking place out of my sight and one gunshot. *Oh, no.*

After more shouts and a torturing amount of time, I heard, "Hey, Noble!"

"Yeah?"

"We got 'em. Come on over!"

Chapter 28

It took all day to give our statements in Jacksonville Thursday because after the preceding day there was more to tell. Chase turned over all the pictures and film he had taken on the swamp and the boat, plane, and drugs were transported by the Coast Guard to Bunner's headquarters. He had good cases against a lot of people by linking them to the drugs and a special bonus connection to a possible kingpin in Miami who was Charlene Luther's father.

Charlene was in the hospital with the gunshot wound Alex had given her when she was shooting at us on the swamp. She almost lost the arm from neglect in getting care.

Tucker was also hospitalized with a shot in the knee when he raised a weapon to try to resist. Alex felt bad about that.

"He'll probably never fully recover from it. There was a lot of damage."

"Don't worry about it," I said. "I would have shot him in the nuts."

"No you wouldn't—you would have missed."

"Well, there would have been a big hole in the side of the barn, anyway."

"Maybe."

* * * *

Mom and Dad got back from the mountains after lunch Saturday and Mom went straight to the kitchen to start cooking when she found out we were all staying in the house. She made us all sit around the kitchen table and we took shifts telling every detail of our adventure. Dad was set up near the back door putting together his new wheelbarrow he picked up at Lowe's on the way back and joined in the conversation after our story was told.

"Alex, you thought any about where you are going to stay? We've got a spare bedroom and you are welcome to stay there." Mom nodded agreement as she put two pans of cornbread in the oven. It was getting about time to eat, according to my stomach.

"No, sir, nothing definite. I thought I might head up toward Macon and see what the possibilities were. I don't want to get into a really big city like Atlanta, but I would like to be close to the things it has to offer."

That was the first he had said anything about his plans, and he had plenty of opportunity after we got back from Jacksonville. Hamp hadn't said much other than what little he contributed to our earlier account of the swamp narrative, but he looked up and spoke.

"Ever been to Athens?"

* * * *

"Think we ought to stop?" I asked.

"We'll regret it if we don't."

Hamp and I were nearing one of the big concrete yard ornament businesses that were outside Folkston. I was driving the Rover, as usual, and Alex was following us in his truck, pulling a Uhaul trailer. After rolling to a stop we got out and headed straight to the area we wanted without telling Alex what was up.

We had been wanting the molded concrete Georgia Bulldog statue that had his hind leg hiked up and plastic plumbing cast through his body, terminating at the end of his pecker. Hook him up to a circulating pump and you've got a continuously peeing dawg. You could also buy an accessory Gator or Yellow Jacket to put under him for a target.

"Gator or Yellow Jacket?" Hamp asked, looking out the corner of his eye at Alex, who was talking to another salesman.

"Hell, let's go with the Gator. He'll just have to get over it." Alex went to the University of Florida. "Besides, your dad would kill us if we got the Jacket."

I left Hamp picking out the pump and plastic pond and followed Alex to his truck. He was packing his purchase among his things so it wouldn't break. It was a fat concrete Gator lying on its back grinning with the image of a Bulldog bulging from its belly. Alex was going to fit in just fine.

"Byron was tickled to be hired on by Chase and his folks," I said for conversation. "Your old job vacancy didn't last long."

"They'll get along fine. How about me—think I'll have any trouble finding a job in Athens? I want to start paying Hamp rent right away."

"Something will come up. In the meantime, I've got a couple of decks to build. Want to help?"

"Sure. I've got a good saw."

"I know."

"Hey Noble?"

"Yeah?"

"'Reach for the fucking sky'?"

Jeez.

0-595-25616-3